DALE MAYER

Merry Mistletoe Madness

Lovely Lethal Gardens 27

MERRY MISTLETOE MADNESS: LOVELY LETHAL GAR-
DENS, BOOK 27
Beverly Dale Mayer
Valley Publishing Ltd.

ISBN-13: 978-1-778864-84-1
Print Edition

Books in This Series:

Arsenic in the Azaleas, Book 1

Bones in the Begonias, Book 2

Corpse in the Carnations, Book 3

Daggers in the Dahlias, Book 4

Evidence in the Echinacea, Book 5

Footprints in the Ferns, Book 6

Gun in the Gardenias, Book 7

Handcuffs in the Heather, Book 8

Ice Pick in the Ivy, Book 9

Jewels in the Juniper, Book 10

Killer in the Kiwis, Book 11

Lifeless in the Lilies, Book 12

Murder in the Marigolds, Book 13

Nabbed in the Nasturtiums, Book 14

Offed in the Orchids, Book 15

Poison in the Pansies, Book 16

Quarry in the Quince, Book 17

Revenge in the Roses, Book 18

Silenced in the Sunflowers, Book 19

Toes up in the Tulips, Book 20

Uzi in the Urn, Book 21

Victim in the Violets, Book 22

Whispers in the Wisteria, Book 23

X'd in the Xeriscape, Book 24
Yowls in the Yarrow, Book 25
Zapped in the Zinnias, Book 26
Merry Mistletoe Madness, Book 27

Boxed Sets and Bundles
https://geni.us/Bundlepage

About This Book

Riches to rags. ... When endings happen, ... new beginnings start. ... Chaos fills the middle!

Can Christmas get any crazier? A new case for Mack and, lucky for Doreen, she finds a cold case connected to it, making her year end on a high note.

All the while she struggles to navigate gift giving and a special party that Nan wants to put on for her at Rosemoor—except Doreen has to solve all kinds of issues, including the missing mistletoe, which Nan insists on having for the party.

And then there are the secrets. Of course it's Christmas, so maybe secrets are to be expected. However, when those secrets involve Nan, maybe Doreen should be worried after all.

Sign up to be notified of all Dale's releases here!
https://geni.us/DaleNews

Chapter 1

First Week of December…

IT WAS EARLY in the evening during the first week of December, and Doreen was curled up in Mack's arms, a blanket wrapped around their shoulders, as they sat by the river, both holding a cup of hot chocolate. Goliath and Mugs were lying beside them, and Thaddeus had curled up under the blanket with them.

"It's getting colder but still no snow. That's unusual for here, according to all the locals," she murmured. "I can't believe Christmas is around the corner."

"And getting closer." Mack laughed. "And you're inundated in party preparations, aren't you?"

"I am." She chuckled. "Not sure how I was conned into doing a lot of the preparations for a party that's being given in my honor though." She shook her head. "After more than a decade of no Christmas in any form while I was married, I have to admit that I'm enjoying myself."

"And it's keeping you out of trouble, so it works for me too."

She punched him lightly in the arm. "Amazing to think that peace and goodwill may preside over the holidays. Yet I thought I read somewhere about violent crime rates rising over main holidays."

"I think that's true. It's stressful for many people. Anytime there is added stress, then eruptions occur."

"True, but, in my mind, a surprise stabbing because someone didn't get a diamond ring, when they live on an instant-noodles income, isn't quite the same."

He nodded. "Maybe not. But what about the young man who wants to buy his girlfriend a diamond ring but can't afford it, so he goes on a crime spree to get the money to buy it?"

"If that's what's required to keep her love, then, first, it wasn't love and, second, she isn't worth ruining his life over. But I get your point." She twisted to look up at him. "You don't have a new case, right? You're not just keeping it from me?"

"Nope, no new case." He tucked her closer to him, pulling the blanket around her shoulders. "And that's a good thing, as we have a mess of paperwork to do. Someone keeps solving the cold cases we have backed up, as well as meddling in current cases. I have to tell you, this person is good, but she's there for the excitement. Yet the puzzling part is, unfortunately she's always there for that dangerous end too. However, when it comes to the cleanup, … she's nowhere to be found."

She turned to him in outrage. "You know I would be if I could be."

His laughter rolled down the stream and then grew louder.

"*Shh*. You're making too much noise."

"We're hardly disturbing anyone."

At that, a loud snort sounded behind them.

She turned at the noises that followed, surmising Richard was propping his chair against the back fence and poking his head over the top. "Good evening, Richard. Isn't it a nice evening out?"

His gaze widened. "Are you nuts? It's friggin' cold out here. It's December, in case you don't have a calendar." He cast one more glance at them and then disappeared down on the other side, mumbling something about crazy people.

She burst out laughing. "Have a good night," she called back to him, struggling to stifle her giggles.

When Richard slammed his door, even Mack joined in with her laughter.

His phone rang just then. Shifting the blanket to find his phone, Mack checked the number, then stood and walked a few steps away. "Mack here. What's up?" He listened for a moment, then turned to look at Doreen.

That was a signal she absolutely recognized. She moved Thaddeus to her shoulder and rose, with the blanket wrapped around the two of them.

"Did you say, mistletoe?" Mack asked.

She froze at that and turned to face Mack in delight.

His frown deepened as he glared at her. "No, sir. … Yes, sir. You're correct. I'll be right there."

She beamed at him. "Mistletoe?"

"Yeah, but it doesn't concern you." He walked closer, adding, "Yet it does mean I have to leave. So Merry Christmas and all that stuff."

"Shouldn't it be *Merry Mistletoe* this time?"

He spun to look at her. "What did you say?"

"*Merry Mistletoe*," she repeated. "Makes a great case name."

"Oh no you don't. If I let you anywhere near this one, it

would be madness." He shook his head and nudged her toward the house. "Time to go inside, as I have to leave."

"I could stay outside," she protested but more just for form, as without his incredibly radiating body heat, she was already starting to shiver. Then she stopped and laughed. "That's even better."

"What is?" he asked, as they reached the patio.

"*Merry Mistletoe Madness*," she crowed.

He stopped to glare at her. "Nice try. It's a current case. Nothing cold about this one."

"So maybe it's time I move into current cases," she suggested, her eyebrows lifting and lowering in a Groucho Marx move.

"Heck no." He opened the back door, moved the clan inside, before locking and closing it behind them. He picked up his keys and headed to the front door.

"It has a lovely ring to it," she called out. When he glared at her, she batted her eyes at him, a big grin on her face.

"Oh, no." With a headshake, he gave her a quick kiss and was gone.

She stepped out on the front porch. "*Merry Mistletoe Madness* it is!"

Richard poked his head out his front door. "Anything to do with you and mistletoe would make anyone mad." And, with that, he retreated and slammed his door.

Unperturbed, Doreen walked inside, with joy in her heart. She had no clue what was happening in terms of murder and mistletoe, but it meant one thing. There was a new case. All she had to do was tie a cold case to Mack's current case, and then she was in! With that thought uppermost in her mind, she had to figure out her next move.

Chapter 2

"No?" Doreen repeated, frowning at Mack. He had stopped by this morning for a cup of coffee, before heading to work. He always greeted her animals with a hug or a scratch behind the ears or a soft touch. She got a hug too, but that didn't deter her.

Mack looked at her, a hint of a smile on his face. She glared at him, her hands on her hips. He shook his head. "Getting mad at me won't change anything." He bopped her gently on the nose. "You know the rules."

"But you could change the rules," she replied in a pleading tone. "I haven't found anything that connects me to this case."

"I know." He beamed. "I've got to admit I like an awful lot about that."

Her shoulders slumped. "You could at least throw me a bone."

"A bone?" he repeated in astonishment. "A bone to you is something completely different and would get me in major trouble."

She raised both hands in frustration. "But then I can't work on your current case, not without a cold case to tie in with it."

"I know," he agreed, with an even bigger grin. "So just think. I get to work this case on my own."

"You'll need my help," she stated, and then she grinned. "I could just wait until you ask for help."

He sighed. "I get that you've become a force unto yourself, but we did have a very successful department before you came to town. You do know that, right?"

"I know," she muttered, and her smile fell away. "I'm bored."

He looked at her. "How can you possibly be bored with all the arrangements Nan appears to be getting into for this party?"

Something in his tone was ever-so-slightly off. Doreen winced. "Has she asked for your help too? I told her that I could handle it, … that you were busy and to leave you alone."

He faced her, and half a smile peeped out. "You can tell Nan whatever you want," he began, "but you and I both know Nan does exactly what she thinks she should do. No one tells her to do anything."

"You won't get an argument from me on that point," Doreen conceded, with a sigh. "I am sorry though. She must be getting in your face."

"You mean, like you're getting into my face?" he asked, raising his eyebrows.

"I'm not though," she protested. "I'm just trying to lend assistance. How could you be suspicious of that?"

He groaned. "And here we are again. Believe it or not, we were doing just fine investigating and solving crimes before you ever showed up in Kelowna."

"I understand that," she admitted, "and I'm really not

trying to make it sound as if you can't do your job without me. Honestly, if I were to be truthful," she began, as she cracked her knuckles, giving away that she was on edge, "it's me who can't do without you guys."

He stopped and frowned at her. "Don't you have anything else to do?" he asked, a little bit of worry creeping into his tone.

"Not really." She shrugged. "It seems as if nothing is going on right now. And how is that even possible?" she muttered. "I mean, I don't want to look forward to a case that's dangerous or edgy and could get me into all kinds of trouble." The problem with that statement was how she couldn't keep the hope out of her tone as she said it.

Mack shook his head. "You, my dear, have a problem."

"I have a problem because I don't have a case to work on," she exclaimed, showing her palms, "and you could help with that."

"No, I can't." He leaned over and kissed her, before she had a chance to reply. "I have to get to the office. I just popped in to see how you were doing."

"I'm fine," she muttered in a forlorn tone.

He burst out laughing. "That won't work on Mugs, and it sure as heck won't work on me. Besides, you told me how you have all that estate stuff to deal with."

She shuddered. "Yeah, and do you have any idea how much all that requires? It's all about intense tiny details," she muttered. "I mean, it's all signatures and documents and statements and dates. There's a lot to it."

"You'll be a wealthy woman now," he pointed out, "so you need to look after it."

"I know, and I've got to find somebody I trust to help. Normally that would be Nan, but she told me that I should pick someone younger," she noted, with a shiver. "That's a bit of a challenge too."

"As much as I hate to even say it, I have a suggestion. *Bernard.*"

She had met him a while back on one of her cases and knew that Mack didn't particularly like him, but he had money and seemed to be level-headed in his approach to life and living and spending versus investments. Plus, she found out with a little internet searching how he donated money to those less fortunate. So, in theory, he could help her sort out her money issues or at least point her in the right direction, maybe recommending a financial advisor. "Oh, that's a good thought."

"I know. I just don't like the idea of your hanging around with him. He is quite the character."

She smiled. "If you don't have anything else for me to do, I might as well talk to him about how to manage my money. He should know what I need to do with all I'm getting from Mathew's estate."

"Is it really such a challenge?" Mack asked, amused. "I mean, most people wouldn't consider having this kind of money a problem."

"Sure, it's not a problem now to pay my bills," she noted, rolling her eyes. "Yet it is a bit of a challenge on how to protect it, how to make it grow into a bigger nest egg, how to help others without my going broke, and that's the difference here. I don't ever want to be poor again, and I want to have money set aside for Nan, as needed. Plus, I want to confirm that I can also help other people. However, I don't know how to manage all that without getting hit with a ton of taxes," she noted, frowning. "The tax thing ... is just outrageous."

He laughed. "I gather you didn't have anything to do with tax preparation when you were married."

"No, gosh no. That would have been considered far too complicated for, you know, a female like me."

He grinned at that. "That was your late husband's problem, and, considering he's now six feet deep in the ground, it's hardly a problem for him at all. And, while I won't say I'm happy about his passing because that seems insensitive, I'm really not too upset that he's out of the picture. And I'm really glad your name was cleared in the process of solving his murder, so now we can move on."

"I know." She sighed. "It's been one heck of a year."

"It certainly has," he agreed. "You could also ask Nick about financial planners he could recommend."

She grimaced but nodded. "I wonder why Nan keeps bugging you to help out with the party plans?" she asked.

"Honestly, she's obsessed over this whole party thing."

"Yeah, you're not kidding," he replied, again with a hint of an odd tone.

She gave him a searching gaze. "Are you not telling me something?"

"Nope," he replied, as he walked toward the front door. "I wouldn't dare." When she frowned, he laughed. "Don't you worry about it. I can handle Nan."

"That's good because she seems to think that nobody else can properly execute this party. She also thinks I might need a little bit of help handling you, by the way."

He turned to her, and then real amusement took over his expression. "Are you telling me that she's giving you advice on how to handle me?"

"Yes, something like that," she muttered. "She seems to think that you're so very different from my ex that I won't really understand anything about you. As if I might fail at our relationship or something. It's kind of demoralizing."

"I'm sure she's just doing it because she loves you."

Doreen nodded. "I'm absolutely certain of that. She's been in my corner always, but that doesn't make this part any easier."

He chuckled. "No, I don't imagine it does." He resumed his walk to her front door. "As much as I want to hang around and hear more details on this, I do have to go to work." And, with that, he was gone.

She stood there on her front porch, hands on her hips, as she watched Mack leave, wondering what she did to deserve such a gentle and wise man.

Just then Richard stepped out from his house, frowned at her, and made to move back inside again.

She shrugged. "It's safe enough," she called out.

He looked around hesitantly. "Are you sure? No buses, no nothing?"

"It's almost Christmas," she noted, "so there won't be tour buses."

He frowned at her. "What about the Christmas lights tour buses?"

"Christmas lights tour buses?" she repeated in astonishment. "What does that mean?"

"They go around the neighborhood, showing everybody the fancy lights that people put up."

"I haven't put up any fancy lights," she muttered, then nodded at his house. "Neither have you."

"That's true," he agreed, yet looking delighted for a moment. "I was thinking about putting up a few though."

"I don't think ours would be considered fancy lights"— she indicated both of their homes—"no matter how many we put up. It really won't be an issue for those tour buses to come here."

"Yeah, you say that now," he muttered dolefully. "Then I'll look out one day and be under intense scrutiny from all the neighbors, once they have put up their fancy lights."

She sighed. "The tour buses have been a trial. I'm sorry, Richard."

"Yeah, you should be," he muttered, as he stormed back into his house.

She wasn't sure what he expected or wanted from her. It didn't seem to matter, since he was the same whether things were going well or things were going badly. Maybe he was just a grumpy old man, and nothing could be said or done. He might always be this way, never content, which was probably not far off the mark. Yet she didn't need to become a grumpy old woman to go along with it. Whatever his problem was, it was his problem, not hers.

Chapter 3

BACK INSIDE HER living room now, Doreen noted that the animals followed close behind her every step. When she looked down, even Mugs seemed to be depressed and bored. "I know. It's been weeks since we had a case." She didn't want to sit here, hoping for cases. That would imply wanting people to commit crimes, resulting in more dead bodies showing up. That was not what she wanted, not really. She didn't want to be bored though.

When her phone rang a few minutes later, she stared down and groaned. "Hello, Nan," she answered cautiously.

After a moment of silence, Nan chuckled. "That sounded as if you are very worried about something I might say."

"Not so much worried you might have something to say," Doreen clarified, "but worried you might be asking me to come down and do more preparations."

"I certainly was," she stated briskly. "It is a party for you, after all."

So Doreen owed Nan because the party was for Doreen? "How does that work?" she asked with a note of humor. "I mean, you're the one supposedly putting this party together."

"Sure," Nan agreed, "but it's a lot of work, so that requires you to help."

"I see," she muttered, with a smile playing on her face. But there was no *seeing* at all. There was never any seeing when it came to this stuff, particularly with Nan involved. Still, Doreen might be better off doing something constructive, even if it was for her own party, rather than sitting here doing nothing.

"I agree," Nan replied.

"I didn't say anything."

"No, but you would have," Nan declared cheerfully. "You're much better off coming here and giving us a hand than to sit there and mope."

"Mope," she cried out. "I'm hardly moping."

"Are you sure?" Nan asked, doubt in her tone.

"Of course I'm sure," Doreen declared. "That's not something I would do."

"Maybe not," Nan conceded in a dismissive tone. "Yet we don't really want you to have that opportunity either."

"Good God," Doreen muttered, half to herself.

Nan laughed. "Yes, very good, and you should be thanking Him because He gave you me."

At that, she stared down at the phone and started to laugh. "I can't argue with that because you have been a lifesaver, indeed."

"*Ha.* In many ways you've been our lifesaver. Things have never been so much fun since you arrived in town."

"Maybe," Doreen replied, "but that's not necessarily a good thing."

"Sure, it is," Nan said, with a laugh. "Don't you worry about all those other people. They can go off and do their own thing. You need to enjoy life a little bit."

"Maybe," Doreen muttered. "I have to admit I was wondering about trying some Christmas baking. I think Mack would enjoy it."

"Yeah, and what are you getting him for Christmas?"

Doreen froze and whispered, "*Uh-oh.*"

Nan cried out, "You don't have anything for him?"

"*Um*, nope, I don't have a thing." She frowned. "I guess a gift is expected, isn't it?"

Nan snorted. "Are you serious?"

"Yeah, I am serious, Nan. I don't have anything for him, okay? I wasn't really thinking that was a thing. We're adults after all."

"Yes, you are adults," Nan agreed in exasperation, "but that doesn't mean you're dead. And adults still want gifts." Then she laughed. "Can I assume that means you didn't get me anything either?"

"Oh, criminy." Doreen sank into the nearest living room chair, one of a matching pair. She still hadn't purchased any other furniture yet.

"I'll take that as a yes," Nan noted cheerfully. "Good thing I've given you a heads-up. That gives you at least a week to get something."

"A week," she repeated, staring at her phone in horror. "What can I possibly buy in a week?"

"I don't know," Nan replied, her tone turning crafty. "What am I now? Your Fairy Godmother? Good Lord, you and Mathew really didn't celebrate Christmas at all? Just another reason I loathe the man."

Doreen didn't have a clue how to respond to that, so she just stayed quiet.

"You'll need to figure that out, and soon."

"Maybe you should turn that around and tell me what

you would like."

"I want a surprise." Nan chuckled. "Something that would make me very happy."

"Something that would make you very happy," Doreen repeated in complete bewilderment. "What could that be?"

More silence came, and then Nan added, "You really do need to think about this, dear." And, with that, Nan ended the call. Doreen was still recovering from this revelation when Nan called her back. "By the way, if you're still thinking about baking, shortbreads would be good. We love them down here." And, with that, she ended the call again.

Doreen wondered if that meant, because Nan and the other residents loved those cookies, then Doreen was supposed to bake them some, or if it meant they would get some from the Rosemoor cook, so it wasn't something Doreen needed to worry about. Sometimes Nan was incredibly confusing. Doreen loved her dearly, but, at times, Nan made absolutely no sense.

Doreen contemplated the conversation, searching her phone to see just what went into shortbreads. When she saw the amount of butter required, her eyebrows shot up. Now that was something interesting. Cornstarch too. She went to the cupboards to see just what she might have, knowing that, even if she did have some of it, she wouldn't likely have the full amount or every ingredient. Besides, how many cookies should she make, and could she give Mack cookies for Christmas? Would that be okay? She had money coming now supposedly, so maybe she should buy him something. However, she had no clue what that would even be.

At least baking cookies showed that she was trying hard to make things work and to do things on her own, even if it did sound a little lacking. She was meticulous when it came to detecting and investigating, but Christmas gifts? She had to wonder how the topic had completely escaped her attention up until now. Maybe it was the fact that her husband had never bought her a Christmas gift. As she thought about it, it was probably more because he didn't want to spend the money. Any gifts he had given her were usually when he had made a business deal of some kind, and she never got access to those gifts anyway. They were labeled as investments and put under lock and key.

She hadn't yet sorted out all of his estate issues, and, since probate was happening, it would take some time to get all that resolved. She definitely didn't want any of those old gifts from Mathew anyway. She didn't even want to think about them. Yet she would have to deal with it, no matter how much she wanted to ignore it. Ignoring only went so far, and, when Mack's brother got into the picture, Nick wouldn't let her ignore very much. He was all about taking care of the current issues before the issues became too big. As she had found out recently, some of these issues were already big.

She was checking out shortbread supplies in her cupboards when her phone rang, and she groaned when she saw who it was. "Hey," she greeted Nick.

"Hey," he replied, with a smile in his tone. "I'm trying not to take it personally, but you never sound very happy when I call you."

"It's not that," she clarified. "It's just that you always bring up issues I must deal with, and, just because I have to deal with them, that doesn't make them easy."

"Of course not," he agreed. "But the good news is that, by dealing with them, we get them off your plate … permanently."

She brightened at that. "You mean, there'll be an end to this?"

He chuckled. "Absolutely. There'll definitely be an end to this."

"I'm glad to hear that, but something tells me that's not why you're calling today."

"No, I've got more paperwork for you to deal with. Also these houses are full of material."

"What do you mean by *material?*" Her mind envisioning dry wall, clothing, or any other nonsense her husband could have put to use.

"Not what you're thinking, I'm sure, but they're all full."

"Meaning?" she asked cautiously.

"Meaning, furnishings."

"Oh," she muttered, frowning at that. "What am I supposed to do with that then?"

"That's what I'm asking you," Nick said. "If you still want to sell these homes, do you want to sell them furnished or empty?"

She sighed. "That makes sense, but it's not today's issue, is it?"

"No, it's not necessarily today's issue," he replied a bit indignant, "but it is an issue we need to plan for. Doreen, don't be afraid of making a decision. There is no right or wrong answer here, just more about your preference."

"Right," she muttered.

He started to chuckle. "I had no idea that you would be so difficult at this stage," he shared, amusement rolling through his tone.

"It's not that I'm being difficult," she clarified, "but if it isn't something I have to deal with right now, then ... you know."

"So, … what is so important in your life right now that you're struggling to answer a few questions and to give me a hand trying to figure out what you want to do with all this stuff? You need to deal with this, Doreen, and you need to do it soon."

She thought about it for a moment and then asked, "What should I get your brother for Christmas?"

The softest of chuckles slipped through the phone. "Interesting," he murmured.

"What's interesting?" she grumbled, glaring at the phone as if she had let loose some major secret, and she was the only one who didn't understand it.

"You're more worried about Mack's Christmas gift than you are about what to do with millions of dollars' worth of furnishings?"

She gasped. "Did you say millions of dollars?"

"Considering the number of houses he's got and the amount of furnishings he's filled them with, I should hope so. Some of them have incredibly expensive paintings."

"Oh, well, we can auction off furniture and artwork, and we already know somebody we can get to handle it all. Scott at Christie's. Have them cart off what they want for auction and leave anything else behind to make the house look lived in."

"Right, that's not a bad idea. I can hire a local Realtor to show Mathew's places and to deal with Scott and his people. A lot of Mathew's acquisitions would probably have provenance, and it appears to be quite the art collection Mathew was working on."

"I think he was collecting some of it when I was there," she said, trying to sound businesslike, but it rattled her. "I never really knew the artists, but maybe some were by

Picasso and Rembrandt."

He whistled. "See? I need this kind of input from you. I'll dig further into these collections because, if that's the case, … that's millions more."

"Oh, … does that mean millions more questions and answers?" She could almost see him shaking his head on the other end of the call.

"You really don't care about money, do you?" Nick asked.

"I care about money in the sense that I have enough to get by," she explained. "I don't care about money in terms of buying apparently valuable paintings that I don't even particularly like."

"Can you think of any you do like?" he asked curiously.

"Nope, but then I haven't had a chance to really see much in the way of art."

"And yet you lived with some of these pieces."

"Sort of, but they were all stuffed in temperature-controlled fancy rooms, and, if I went in there, Mathew always hovered. So it's not as if I got a chance to really see anything."

"Right," Nick noted, humor lacing his tone. "Do you want to keep anything? We found lots of jewelry in his main residence."

"Oh, right." She groaned. "Am I supposed to care about that stuff?"

"No, you don't have to care about any of it. But, if you do care about it, this is the time to speak up, so we can set aside what you want to keep versus what you want to sell at auction."

"I don't think I care about any of it," she replied. "If any are pieces he gave to me, I wouldn't have been allowed to have them anyway."

"Meaning?"

"Meaning that they had to be kept in the safe all the time. Mathew required it all to be locked up all the time, so what is the point of having jewelry I can't even wear?" She thought it was a reasonable question.

Nick laughed. "I won't argue with you on that, but your response is definitely different."

So she assumed he didn't agree. "I am absolutely different," she said crossly, "but I don't know if you're trying to tell me whether that's good or bad."

"I'm not telling you either way," Nick pointed out. "I'm just telling you that these things are yours to do with what you will. If you don't want anything to do with any of it because of bad memories or whatever reasons, I'm more than happy to help you get rid of it all."

"I would love to get rid of it all," she stated. "Maybe I should take a look at what's there before I make such a blanket statement, but I can't imagine anything there has any meaning to me. Oh, except Nan had given me a necklace at one point in time, and Mathew insisted I get rid of it and not wear it because it just wasn't good enough, as far as he was concerned."

"What a *nice* fellow," Nick quipped.

"*Not*, but, if that happens to be listed in his estate inventory, I would like that. It was Nan's grandmother's necklace."

"Ah, so a family heirloom. So, you want to keep nothing, but you won't make that final decision until we get the estate list, is that correct? Or maybe we should make a trip down there in person. Help you to get clear on what's there."

"I was wondering about that, but I would want Mack

there too. Are you okay with that?"

"I am okay with that, but maybe we should just get a realtor to film the contents, so the three of us don't have to coordinate our calendars," he suggested.

"Yeah, I like that idea."

"Good. I'll arrange that for each of his homes. Also some money is going into your bank account today, if you need something to buy those Christmas gifts with."

"Oh," she muttered.

"Okay, that doesn't sound positive."

"I don't know what to do about Christmas gifts," she admitted, with a sigh. "It's not something we ever did, so it wasn't really on my radar."

"Mathew didn't buy you Christmas gifts?" he asked.

"No, he told me that Christmas was fake and too commercialized and that nobody should be spending money based on a date on the calendar. It was just this big commercial exercise that was a lost cause."

"I won't argue regarding the commercialization of it because that's true. However, it can also be a wonderful time to show people that you love them," he reminded her gently.

"Oh."

At that, he started to laugh again. "And you just need to sort it out, without causing yourself major stress because that would upset Mack completely. So, what it is that you want to give him, or what do you think he would appreciate?"

"I have no idea," she said helplessly.

"Yes, you do," Nick encouraged her. "You absolutely do. Don't think in terms of money, don't think in terms of need, just think in terms of something he might like." And, with that, he ended the call.

Chapter 4

DOREEN GLARED INTO the phone, wondering how everybody could have such a specifically useful way to view things, yet she felt as if she had absolutely no clue about anything. She had stepped outside to talk to Nick, wandering her garden while discussing Mathew's estate. It was so cold out here that she was now chilled.

Swearing slightly, she headed inside to her kitchen and put on the teakettle. She and Mack had not mentioned anything about exchanging Christmas gifts, so maybe it wasn't supposed to be a big deal. It would be hard to think of what she could do that wouldn't be considered cheap, especially now that she supposedly had some money. She did have the ability to buy things, but she didn't think that would be what Mack cared about. Then again, maybe she was wrong. Maybe he did care.

She groaned at that and then brightened. Her husband had kept a collection of watches, so maybe that would be something to consider. Yet she had no idea if she could even access those. They weren't something that her husband ever wore. To him they were more of an investment. She remembered one conversation when he'd told her how he had spent some astronomical amount of money on one, and she'd had no idea that a watch could cost that kind of money.

When she had suddenly become single, she considered getting a watch to help bring order to her new and independent life. Yet she'd immediately dumped the idea because of the expected cost. It hadn't taken her too long to figure out that, while some watches were definitely pricy, others were ridiculously priced. At least in her mind because she'd been so broke at the time. Now, however, she could see that, for some people, this was probably a major investment and a type of collecting. She just didn't see the point in a lot of things in life.

She shook her head as she stood in the kitchen and realized that she didn't have all the ingredients needed for shortbread. As she looked closer at the recipe to see what was involved, she figured it wouldn't be so horrifically difficult to make shortbreads. She wondered if homemade cookies would be okay for Mack because it would show a lot of progress on her part. She decided to go to the grocery store, yet probably shouldn't take the animals.

Intellectually it made sense that she couldn't bring them in among the foodstuffs. She laughed as she imagined Thaddeus in the grocery store when she got to the fresh veggies. He would be all over the place, trying to get free samples. Goliath wouldn't appreciate the stampede of people. Mugs would be making friends and interrupting her idea of a quick shopping trip. Plus, there would inevitably be those people walking up to her to exclaim, "You're Doreen. The cold cases lady, with all her animals."

She sighed and decided against taking the animals after all. Just as she was about to get into her vehicle, her phone rang. Doreen checked her screen. "Hey, Wendy. I haven't heard from you in a while.”

“I haven't had a whole lot of reasons to call you, and I don't mean that in a bad way,” she shared. “Yet, just in case you need a little bit of Christmas money, I have a check for you.”

“A check?” Doreen repeated, drawing a blank.

“Yes, the last of the clothing and items from the house have been sold.”

“Oh,” Doreen replied in delight. “I would never say no to that.”

“I didn't think you would.” Wendy chuckled. “So come on down and pick it up anytime.”

“I'm heading to the grocery store right now, so I can swing by your store beforehand.”

“Perfect. If you want, I can convert the check to cash, and you can use that to buy your groceries today.”

“I would love that,” Doreen replied. The poor person inside her head was already lining up just what that would look like in terms of groceries. She knew that mind-set was now silly, but, after being as broke as she had been this year, she couldn't let go of those thoughts that easily. She didn't even know how much money Nick had deposited into her account or even what her previous balance had been. So she would sort that out later.

Doreen drove out onto the street and down to see Wendy, spent a few minutes visiting, and, as she walked out, Wendy asked her, “Have you got any Christmas plans?”

“I do and I don't. Mack and I haven't really discussed that, and I'm really struggling with what to get Mack for Christmas.”

“Ah.” Wendy nodded. “Yeah, that's sometimes a tough one. Is there anything he particularly likes?”

Doreen shrugged. "He enjoys cooking and eating and really likes his coffee. He doesn't have time for hobbies. We like gardening, and he's really good at building patio stuff, but I don't know if he needs tools. I wouldn't seem to be the right person to buy that sort of thing for him."

Wendy laughed. "I get that, but you would be surprised at the things people come up with. Maybe there's a book that he particularly wanted or something else equally fun."

"Maybe." Doreen shrugged. "I have to think about that some more."

Wendy added, "It doesn't have to be new, you know? It could be something you've made that is appreciated way more."

"Yeah, I just don't have any skills." Doreen winced.

"You have a lot more skills than you know, and you've really been putting them to good use helping this town," Wendy noted.

Doreen laughed at that. "My grandmother is determined to throw me a thank-you party next week," she shared.

"I know." Wendy gave her a bright smile. "I got an invitation."

"Really?" she asked, looking at Wendy in delight. "I didn't realize Nan was inviting people."

"Oh boy, I think she's inviting half the town. I will be there," Wendy stated. "I wouldn't miss it. We all have something to thank you for."

"Oh, I don't want that," Doreen muttered in horror. "I would just as soon we skip all that."

Wendy laughed. "You might, but a lot of people want an opportunity to be there and to see you receive thanks for all the work you've done for us."

"Oh, gosh," Doreen muttered, her face hot with embarrassment. She returned to her car, really hoping the party wouldn't be one of those kinds of events. She'd always felt incredibly self-conscious for whoever was in the hot seat, looking as if they were suffering from all the attention.

It was a lovely thing for Nan to do, but it was totally unnecessary. It's not as if Doreen had done all this for the fame or the spotlight to be on her. All the work, all her efforts and everything she'd done was because of the cases, giving closure to the victims' families. The fact that solving a cold case also helped somebody else in the process was just a good thing occurring at the same time.

Groaning at the thought of so many people coming to the party, Doreen wondered if Nan needed help paying for it. As soon as she picked up a few groceries, she headed home and unloaded the groceries. Then she called Nan. "Hey, do you want me to come down today?"

"Absolutely," Nan agreed.

"Do you need some money to help pay for the party?"

"Nope, we've got it in hand," Nan replied. "See you in ten."

Chapter 5

DOREEN QUICKLY GOT the animals ready and herself bundled up, and then the four of them stepped outside and headed toward the path to Rosemoor. She winced as she passed all the cold-case-related places they'd had so many issues with over time, but it seemed as if everybody was being good to each other right now amid the holiday season.

At Rosemoor she walked through the main entrance, with several people calling out greetings to her and her animals. She smiled and waved and headed toward Nan's apartment. As she got there, the door opened, just as she was arriving.

"Don't you tell her now," Richie said, giving Nan a hug before turning to leave.

Doreen stopped, frowned at Nan, and then looked at Richie. "Don't tell me what?" Nan's expression immediately turned innocent, which made her look incredibly guilty.

"We weren't talking about you, dear," Nan replied.

"I don't want you manipulating the staff to make this party happen either."

"I wouldn't do that," she remarked, staring at her granddaughter in astonishment.

Yet Doreen already knew *exactly* how much Nan got herself involved in things just like that. "You might say that"—shaking her head—"but I do know you."

Nan grinned a huge smile and nodded. "And isn't it lovely that you do?" She opened her arms for a hug. "It makes my life so much easier."

Doreen bent to hug her but still sighed. "What are you up to?"

"We're up to nothing," she declared.

Doreen nudged Richie, hoping to get something out of him, but he was having none of it.

"Hello and goodbye," he said, and was gone in a flash.

Doreen frowned at her grandmother, who waved her hand. "It's fine, child. Everything's absolutely fine. Besides, it's the season for secrets." She then spent a few minutes nuzzling the animals, one by one.

"As long as you're not interfering in anything you shouldn't be," Doreen noted, her gaze narrowing.

"Of course not. I would *never*," Nan protested innocently.

Still, it was hard to keep the suspicion out of Doreen's thoughts as she sat down to discuss the party plans with Nan. Something was just so cagey and crafty about her grandmother today that Doreen couldn't quite relax. Currently they were affixing red velvet bows on the pine bough garlands. Her animals were surprisingly well mannered today. Thaddeus sat quietly on her shoulder. Mugs was asleep on the floor by Nan's feet, while Goliath lay on the dining table, his tail occasionally swaying into the garlands and the bows.

When they had done this batch, Doreen asked Nan,

"Are you guys sure you don't need some money to help with this?"

"Of course not," Nan declared, eyeing her askance. "We're all just fine. Rosemoor has a Christmas decorating budget. We have just added a few touches here and there."

"You all might be fine," Doreen muttered in frustration, "but I am not. All you're doing is just reminding me that I don't have anything for Mack," she confessed.

"I told you. Make him shortbreads, dear. That'll make him happy," she stated, with an airy wave of her hand.

"I did just buy the ingredients." At that, Nan turned and looked at her in delight. Doreen shrugged. "I figured I should at least try some Christmas baking on my own."

"You absolutely should try," Nan exclaimed, "but do more than try. You need to succeed." She was openly scolding Doreen now. "Attitude is everything."

Doreen smiled. Her grandmother would lecture her until she was done and would love every minute of it. In the meantime, for Doreen, it was a little hard to realize how far off track she could get at times, but trust Nan to pull her right back into place. "I wasn't thinking I was doing that badly," she protested.

"No, but, when learning something new, you have to keep at it, keep using a skill in order for it to become something you can count on," Nan explained. "So, you can't just bake today and never again. It needs to be an ongoing process."

"Maybe," Doreen replied, "but it's still not a skill that comes easily for me."

"I'm not sure skills are supposed to come easily," Nan clarified, studying her granddaughter. "Natural talents might, but skills? Skills seem to be something completely and altogether different."

"Maybe," Doreen muttered. "Still seems a little off, though."

Nan laughed. "*Off* isn't bad," she pointed out. "In fact, *off* is often good. You just have to accept that what you think is good versus what somebody else may think is good can be a totally different story."

Doreen wasn't here to argue with Nan, and it seemed to be a moot point at this stage anyway. "I'll try the shortbreads, maybe tomorrow," she shared. "God knows I've got nothing else to do."

Nan frowned, looking at Doreen in concern.

"I'm fine." Doreen sighed. "It's just been a while since I had a case, and I'm a little stir-crazy."

"We should be happy about that," Nan noted. "We don't want to constantly have these issues."

"Of course not," Doreen conceded. "I'm wondering if I should just do more volunteering elsewhere."

"You can always help at the food bank and serve Christmas dinner."

"But that only would keep me busy this month. Besides, I want to talk to Mack about that first," she shared. "I don't know whether he has any plans or not, and I don't want to scuttle them by not checking with him first."

"Oh, I do like to hear that," Nan exclaimed, looking at Doreen in delight. "You are learning."

She frowned. "Now, if only I could learn on the topic of this gift-giving thing. Surely I'm not so far off as to be unaware of what Mack would like," she muttered. "Though I must say, you've got me a little worried."

"Oh dear." Nan frowned. "I didn't mean to scare you or to upset you. Your husband really wasn't a nice man. I know we shouldn't speak ill of the dead, but he really did a number on you."

Doreen shook her head. "You've done nothing but speak ill of him anyway," she shared, "so the fact that he's dead doesn't make a whole lot of difference."

"I just don't want you to do anything that would cause you to lose Mack."

"Cause me to lose Mack?" Doreen repeated, staring at Nan. "You really think that I'll do something as drastic as that?"

"No, I'm not thinking that at all," she replied, with a pat of Doreen's hand. "However, I've been around a little bit longer than you and understand that it's pretty easy to do the wrong thing. It's not a one-and-done thing. It's a relationship. Just when you thought everything was nice and tidy, you realize that you haven't sorted out something major, and now it's a big thing that you didn't realize was a thing at all." After sharing that convoluted mess, Nan smiled at Doreen. "But enough of that talk, we have work to do." Nan pointed to her amazing work list of everything that needed to be done for the party.

Doreen stared at her. "Are you doing this all by yourself?" she asked in astonishment.

"No, of course not," she said, with another dramatic wave of her hand. "We have lots of volunteers. But the fact remains that we don't want to leave it for too many people to mess up," Nan pointed out. "So we need to keep a close eye on it."

"Right." Doreen shook her head. "When you mentioned it would be here at the center, I assumed management was okay with it."

"Of course they are," Nan declared, frowning at her.

"And, yes, we did talk to them."

"Are you sure?"

Nan laughed. "Of course we did. The last thing we want is something to go wrong at that stage and have management all upset because we didn't include them in our plans."

"Yeah, that wouldn't go over well, would it?" Doreen noted, staring at Nan. "And you're sure you're not up to something?"

Nan gave her that mostly innocent, yet somehow guilty look, then asked, "Oh, my dear, what could we possibly be getting into?"

"I don't know," Doreen admitted, narrowing her gaze. "The fact that you're even *this* involved has me worried."

She chuckled. "Trust, child. You just need a little more trust."

"Ah, well." Doreen groaned, staring at her grandmother. "I might need *a lot* more trust. A whole lot."

"You better find it then," Nan stated. "I don't have time for any of that now."

"*Right,*" Doreen muttered, not exactly sure what she was getting herself involved in.

"You go along now," Nan said dismissively. "You have to find mistletoe."

"What do you mean?" Doreen asked.

Nan frowned, shaking her head. "You heard about the semi-truck accident, right?"

"No, I didn't." She looked over at Nan.

"Oh." Nan gave her half a smile. "Mack's really keeping you out of this one, isn't he?"

She eyed her grandmother in astonishment. "Until now I didn't know that he's trying to keep me out of anything, but you're not helping by giving me bare-bones explanations."

"I really don't want to get too involved. That would upset Mack."

"As if you care about that." Doreen snorted.

"Of course I care. He's a very special man, after all," she said, "and I don't want us to do anything that'll mess up his plans."

"Oh. goodness." Doreen sighed, staring at her grandmother. "Please stay out of Mack's life, Nan."

"I would love to," she agreed in that same rumbling comfortable tone that she oozed all the time—when she wanted something. "I mean, it would be so much easier if people would pay attention and would do what they're supposed to do."

"Oh boy," Doreen muttered, "Nan, please, please, just leave Mack alone."

Nan shook her head. "I have no intention of getting involved with Mack at all." And, with that, Nan went off in peals of laughter.

Her grandmother's glee just made Doreen feel even worse. She didn't know how to get Nan to butt out of Mack's life. The last thing Mack needed was her grandmother's interference, particularly if he was working a case. "And you do know that I'm not allowed to involve myself in any case that isn't connected to a cold case."

"That's true," Nan confirmed. "So, we'll have a problem, won't we?"

"I don't know that we'll have a problem at all," Doreen noted, shaking her head at Nan. "I don't understand what could possibly be a problem."

"That's a good thing," Nan declared, with a bright smile. "We definitely don't want problems at this stage."

"You're talking in circles," Doreen muttered. "Please, if you've got something to say about whatever is going on, let's hear it."

"I can't, my dear. It's Christmas, which is all about secrets."

"Oh my gosh, I'll have to apologize to Mack for you butting into his life, won't I?"

"I don't know." Nan faced her with those bright blue eyes, almost chortling with laughter. "Will you?"

Doreen groaned. "Yeah, … I will. So I might as well do it upfront because I can't stop you from whatever madness you're involved in."

"It's not madness," she argued. "It's just that sometimes … people need a little help. That's all."

"Right, and you think Mack needs help? Remember that, if you get me in trouble over any of his current cases, I won't be allowed to work on any cold cases anymore." She hated to admit it, but it would completely ruin the fun she had on a day-to-day basis.

"No, no, of course not," Nan agreed, staring at her in astonishment. "We wouldn't want that to happen. We have just as much fun with your cases as you do."

"Right," Doreen said, realizing at least that much was the truth coming from Nan. "So, you won't do anything to mess this up?"

"No, of course not," Nan declared, with a bright smile. A *too* bright smile. Somehow that didn't make Doreen feel any better. She frowned when Nan patted her hand and added, "You go chase down that mistletoe. We have to have it, and that is not negotiable."

"It's an old folks home, Nan. It's not as if everyone is doing any kissing anyway," Doreen noted, with an eye roll.

Nan narrowed her eyes at her granddaughter. "I hope we all are kissing for the rest of our lives. Remember, Doreen. Romance is never dead, no matter how old you are, child."

"Does that mean that you and Richie are still an item?"

"Mind your own business, dear."

Doreen didn't know what to say to that, but she certainly didn't want to think about this place erupting in loud smooches at Christmas, or any other time, that's for sure. "Fine. What is it you want me to do?"

"Find some mistletoe for the Rosemoor party. Maybe a sprig for your own house too, right? Then go make yourself busy." Nan stood, brushing her away. "You need to look after yourself. Maybe get a haircut. And I don't know, go get a massage or something," she suggested hopefully.

Doreen stared at her, then shook her head. "*Nah*. I'm fine."

"Oh, good. And your hair?"

"My hair is fine," she replied, staring at her awkwardly, "unless you're trying to tell me something."

"No, my dear, I would never do that," Nan declared.

"Yes, you would," Doreen admitted, sighing. "I don't think I'll like Christmas celebrations much if it comes with this much focus on me, learning how to be like everyone else."

Nan laughed. "You just be you, and you'll love it," she said warmly. "You must allow yourself to open up and to enjoy it."

And if that wasn't enough to set her nerves on edge, Nan's follow-up words caused Doreen to nearly recoil with horror.

"Of course it depends on Mack too, you know?"

"How about we leave Mack out of it," Doreen said.

"Don't be bothering him, Nan. If you need anything, just tell me, and we'll deal with it."

"I will. I will. I will," she declared, with that same innocent yet horribly guilty look in her eye. The laughter in her expression was enough to get Doreen's blood pressure rising. Nan immediately noticed. "You, my dear, need to go get some rest. Just go home, relax, make your shortbreads, and have a couple too," she suggested, with a bright smile. "Absolutely no point in baking if you don't enjoy the end product. That's half the fun."

"I struggle with eating anything I bake, as I'm half afraid I'll poison myself."

Nan frowned at her and then peeled off in joyful laughter. "I do enjoy your visits," she admitted, with a bright smile. "So I hate to say it, but you need to get going," Nan stated in no uncertain terms. After another reference to Christmas surprises and all that, Doreen and her animals were unceremoniously bumped out of Nan's apartment.

Doreen hadn't even been offered tea or any treats, and neither had her animals. Even their cuddles had been held to a minimum. Her grandmother was really caught up in whatever she was into, and it would definitely be interesting to learn more about that. The good thing was that her grandmother was also completely engaged in the planned party and having a lot of fun in the process, and Doreen would never take that away from her. Of anybody she had ever met, Nan appeared to be enjoying retirement and taking advantage of all the activities Rosemoor had to offer.

When you were eighty-plus, did you truly know how to live life? Did your dreams come true? Did retirement living morph into truly living? Doreen didn't know, but Nan was certainly enjoying her senior years more than anybody else

Doreen knew. Actually Nan always seemed to be enjoying her life, no matter her age. Yet, at Rosemoor, Nan appeared to have a whole new lease on life and had no intention of giving it up anytime soon.

And, with the shortbread recipe now her focus, Doreen and her animals headed home.

Chapter 6

WHEN MACK STOPPED by at the end of the day, Doreen greeted him at the door with a cookie. He raised one eyebrow and opened his mouth for a bite. She popped in a morsel, and he chewed it with a frown.

"Shortbread?" he asked cautiously.

She frowned back at him. "It doesn't taste like shortbread?" she asked doubtfully. "I've never had any, so I don't know."

He just nodded and chewed a little bit more.

"Okay, *great*," she muttered. "Somehow I managed to mess that up too."

"I don't know that you messed it up," he clarified, "but you do realize that shortbread needs a light hand, right? This cookie still tastes good," he added.

She glared at him. "But not *that* good, so *not* a light hand."

"I'm not sure what you did," he replied, "but shortbreads should be just a quick mix, a quick roll, and then pop it into the oven."

"*Hmm. …* Good to know. I did buy enough ingredients, so maybe I should try it again."

He walked into the kitchen behind her, snagged up another shortbread cookie from the counter, and nodded. "I have to have another bite to be sure."

She glared at him. "If you're having another bite, it can't be that bad."

"Nope, it's not," he said, with a snort. "It just needs a little … practice."

"How come everything I do needs a little practice?" she asked, a forlorn note evident in her tone.

He turned and looked at her. "You're really having a tough day of it, *huh*?"

"I shouldn't be, though," she muttered. "I mean, everything should be fine."

"Should be, but is it?"

"Nan did tell me to go track down some mistletoe," she shared, "but I don't know anything about it. She seems to think she is missing some mistletoe."

His lips twitched. "I think you may find that any missing mistletoe is more missing in Nan's head than anywhere else," he muttered.

"She should know that a cutting of fresh mistletoe lasts one month, and so we have to get more each year." Doreen turned to face Mack. "She also seemed to think that you hadn't told me about a case."

He froze in the act of popping a third shortbread into his mouth, his eyes widening. "Oh, did she now?" he muttered.

"Yeah." She studied him carefully. "You wouldn't do that, would you?"

"You and I both know how much we enjoy sharing cases," he replied. "We also know that I can only share so much with you about a pending investigation. So, no, I wouldn't hold back *case* info deliberately."

"But," she noted, hearing the inflection in his wording, "something appears to be going on that I don't know about."

He smiled. "It is Christmas, remember?"

"Which is exactly what Nan told me," Doreen cried out in frustration. "I don't know if you guys realize how little I know about celebrating Christmas." When Mack frowned at her, she shrugged. "Mathew didn't want anything to do with it, and it's been a very long time since I had any family nearby. Nan cared about me, and she still does, but she was also living her best life with her carefree lifestyle at that point, rather than focusing her days on her married granddaughter," she muttered. "So honestly, when it comes to Christmas, I really don't know what is expected."

"Nothing's expected," he replied. "It should be just a fun time to celebrate. People have various traditions, so it's a little different for everyone, depending on what they are used to."

"What about gifts? I don't have a clue."

"If you want to give me something," he suggested, "then feel free. Otherwise I am not bothered."

"Yeah, but that just means you'll turn around and get me something, and then I'll feel bad because I don't have something to reciprocate." When he burst out laughing, she nodded. "But I'm right, aren't I?"

"I don't know," he said, with a smile. "I can tell you right now that I don't have anything specifically Christmas-related for you at this time."

"But you do have something for me," she noted, latching onto his wording again.

"I do, yes," he agreed, "but it's not meant to stress you out. That's the opposite of my intent." When she glared at him, he just smiled. "Honestly."

"Sure, *honestly*," she muttered. "It seems as if everybody is involved in something that I don't know anything about."

He stared at her. "You, my dear, are at the heart of everything, as always," he shared. "So maybe this time you can just step back a bit."

"But what's this about missing mistletoe?"

"We had that vehicle crash, remember?"

"No, I don't remember. You didn't tell me about a crash."

He frowned. "The night that we were sitting at the river."

"No, you didn't mention a crash," she pointed out. "You had to leave, and it had something to do with mistletoe, but you didn't tell me what it was about, not then and not afterward either."

"Okay, sorry. We had a semi-truck crash on the highway, bringing in poinsettias and a lot of Christmas-themed plants and flowers. Honestly, it's a little late for them to be trucked in, but it was the overflow from Vancouver, after our local crop had not survived the freezing temps we had here earlier. Anyway, the driver had a bad accident, and the entire load was either stolen or left behind to be damaged by the elements, during another of the cold snaps we've had. So all the live plants were just gone."

"Oh, I see. So it's not that the mistletoe is missing. It's just that the town doesn't have any."

"Exactly. So, everything in Kelowna has been pretty well wiped out, and people are scrambling to get any poinsettias and a bunch of other stuff from nearby towns. I can't say it's ever been anything I particularly worried about."

"Okay," she muttered.

"Feel better?"

"Yes, … it's always tough when it feels as if I'm being excluded from something."

"You know that's just a part of Christmas," he said, dropping a kiss on her nose. "Christmas is full of secrets."

"Yeah, but I don't like secrets and surprises," she declared.

He burst out laughing. "It doesn't seem to matter because, when Christmas happens—short of people setting out how they want to handle it ahead of time, like families or people in a relationship—Christmas is full of all kinds of things, and they don't have to be bad, even if secrets or surprises." When she looked at him in disbelief, he shook his head. "You know, if that husband of yours wasn't dead already, I would pound him into the ground right now."

"Take a number," she muttered. "I think I could find enough reasons to do that myself. I did talk to your brother again."

"Good. Is he coming through with the paperwork?"

"Yeah, but he just brought up another big mess of issues though," she muttered.

"Such as?"

"Mathew's houses were full, so Nick asked me what I wanted to do with all the furnishings. He did mention that sometimes it's easier to sell houses if they looked lived in."

"That's very true. Isn't that what *staging* is all about?" he asked, with a nod. "So just leave the furnishings as is, until the houses sell, right?"

"That's what I suggested, but then Nick mentioned valuable paintings."

Mack slowly turned from where he'd been eyeing the cookies, and she had to laugh because he seemed to be very seriously thinking that cookie number four was due.

"You know the cookies can't be *that* bad."

"Nope, they're not bad at all, just a little bit more of a chew factor than I was expecting, that's all, but they taste just fine."

"Chew factor," she repeated, "Right. So, in other words, they're tough."

"I'm really not sure how that works," he said apologetically. "I've never had tough shortbread before."

"Yeah, well, if there was a way to make it happen, you can count on me for that," she muttered.

"What do you mean by expensive paintings?" he asked, facing her.

She shrugged. "Mathew collected art."

"Of course he did." Mack sighed.

Doreen nodded. "As far as I can tell, he was really proud of it."

"And do you know what's in his collection?"

"I don't. I was never allowed to look at it very much. If I did, I had to say the right thing. Otherwise he would get quite pissed off because I never said the right thing. I learned it was best to just avoid the whole issue."

His lips twitched. "I can see that."

"Yeah, well, *anyway*, I told Nick that we should probably contact the same auction people as before and sell them."

"Oh, that's a good idea. At least you have a trusted connection there you can work with."

"That's what I thought." She nodded. "Nick seemed to think that was a decent idea too."

"I'm sure he did." Mack smiled. "He's pretty reasonable when it comes to that kind of thing, isn't he?"

"I think so," she muttered. "Anyway, he'll get a realtor to list everything in the houses. In fact, he wants the realtor to film the contents of all the houses. That way we don't have to fly out there and see each house and everything firsthand, before selling them. Scott would appreciate a visual record too, but I'm sure he'll want to send somebody out there in person as well. If he wants me there too, I think you should go with me—if you could get one whole day off to do that sort of thing."

"Interesting." He absentmindedly shifted his watch.

"Is that watch bothering you?" she asked, noticing his irritated skin.

He shrugged. "The wristband is old. I've been meaning to get a new one but just haven't gotten around to it."

She tucked away that information, wondering if she should try to find something in her husband's collection or if that would just piss off Mack. She seemed to walk through a mine field these days. Was it okay to give Mack a watch that came from her late husband's collection? The very same ex who had tried to kill her? She would talk to Mack's brother and see if that was okay to regift or would be something so wrong that Mack would be angry.

"Anyway, I can tell you this about my current case," Mack began, as he walked closer to her. "The mistletoe on that truck died or was taken, so now we have no live mistletoe in town."

"Which I'm sure is upsetting a lot of people," Doreen noted. "It's driving Nan completely batty."

He laughed. "Anything that doesn't go the way Nan wants it to go is practically guaranteed to drive her batty."

Doreen laughed. "I was down there earlier, and so much hush-hush stuff was going on that, when Nan pushed me out the door, I was happy to leave."

He looked at her askance. "Seriously? What are they up

to?"

"I don't know," she muttered. "And I think it's better if I don't know at this stage." He looked at her worriedly, and she nodded. "I know. I know. She's my grandmother, but you also may want to talk to Darren about his grandfather."

Mack laughed. "Darren is trying very hard to avoid his grandfather right now, as Richie is constantly getting Darren in trouble."

"I feel the same way about Nan," Doreen muttered. "Yet, as long as everybody at Rosemoor is doing okay, I guess we can leave them to their own mess. They are adults, after all."

"If you say so," Mack conceded.

"Anyway, you're not getting me something for Christmas, right?"

He frowned and asked cautiously, "Are you saying you don't want anything for Christmas?"

She frowned right back at him. "I was thinking that maybe we really didn't need to do gifts, you know?"

"We don't *need* to do gifts," he clarified, "but I did have something in mind I wanted to get you."

She stared at him. "How come everybody always seems to have something in mind, but I don't even understand how the system works?"

"That's because you're overthinking it," he said gently. "The only thing that matters is that, if you want to give somebody a gift, you give it to them for the right reason."

"And that is?"

"Because you want to," he stated.

She smiled. "Okay, I think I can handle that."

He twisted his watchband again and frowned. "This is really irritating."

"Maybe that's something I could look for," she suggested.

"A watchband?" Looking down at it, he nodded. "Sure, why don't you buy me a new watchband for Christmas. That'll give you something that will make you feel good to give me because it's something I need, and I know how much you appreciate that."

"Right." Still, she frowned. "Yet I don't know if it's something I can do though."

"There is a size involved," he noted, and he quickly wrote it down on the notepad she kept nearby. "Even if not for Christmas, maybe you could spend a minute researching to find me one that won't irritate my skin."

"I think it has to do with the coating on them," she muttered.

"Yeah, maybe. The coating has probably worn off on this one."

"You can always get a gold one or something," she pointed out, frowning at the size of it, how it was loose on his wrist.

"Gold?" he repeated and laughed. "Yeah, that's not happening. I wouldn't even know what to do with it."

"Wear it, of course."

He smiled, tapped her on the nose, and said, "How about some food, before I finish all the rest of your cookies?"

"They can't be that bad then."

"They aren't bad at all," he replied. "They've got a really good flavor."

"So just high on the chew factor then?"

His grin flashed. "Exactly, just a high chew factor, and that's a good thing."

"How on earth is that a good thing?"

"Because you taught me something new."

"What's that?" she asked, glaring at him, knowing it wouldn't be something she liked.

He laughed. "I didn't know that shortbread came chewy."

She sighed. "I'll try again."

"You do that," he said, as he reached for another.

She smacked his hand. "Didn't you say you wanted dinner first? Did we make dinner plans?" She stared at him in astonishment.

He sighed. "I thought we did. You were supposed to make chicken."

"Oh. I don't think I got the memo."

"Ah." He shrugged. "Pizza?"

"Pizza would be great," she replied. "I guess I should have taken the chicken out to thaw, *huh?*"

"You didn't though, so it's no big deal."

"I don't feel like cooking tonight," she grumbled in frustration. "I think something is wrong with me." He looked at her, raising one brow. She shrugged. "I never really feel like cooking. It isn't something that comes naturally in any way. It's not a skill that I can just turn around and say, *Hey, this is something I can do*, without feeling like it's a chore."

"Because it's a chore that you want to get out of doing."

"I hate to put it that way," she muttered.

He shrugged. "It just is what it is. Nobody said you had to cook all the time. Nobody said I had to cook all the time either. The good news is, we can do whatever we want most of the time." And, with that, he pulled out his phone and ordered pizza. As he put away his phone, he nodded. "Twenty minutes."

"Oh, good," she said, as her stomach rumbled.

He smiled. "Have you tried any of your cookies?"

"No, I was worried."

"Worried?" he asked.

"Yeah. What if they weren't edible?"

He nodded. "I can assure you that they're edible." He snagged another one. "Quite edible."

"You need to stop," she protested, "or you won't have any room for dinner."

"Really?" he asked, with an eye roll. "Do you honestly think that argument will work with me?"

"I don't know. You would think so," she muttered. "Apparently that's how people do it with kids."

"I'm hardly a kid," he pointed out, with a laugh.

"That's part of the reason Nan is so worried about me."

"What do you mean?"

She sighed. "Nan mentioned something today that I'm struggling with."

"*Uh-oh*. Nan's very good at saying all kinds of things."

"I know, but she seems to think I'm in danger of losing you. If I don't do certain things, I'll mess it up somehow, and you'll walk away from me."

He stopped midbite, then walked over to her and tugged her close and just held her. "I don't think Nan has any good advice in that department," he murmured gently. "Next time she tries to give you any relationship suggestions, just tell her that you'll figure it out, just as you figure out everything else."

"Do you think so?" she asked, leaning back to look up at him, hating the insecurity overtaking her. "I never quite know what to say when she gets in that mood."

"Of course you don't," he agreed. "Nan is absolutely lovely, and I know where she's coming from, and it's okay."

He leaned down and gave Doreen a kiss. "Now put that thought out of your mind and let's deal with more important things."

"What's that?" she asked.

"My stomach." Then he burst into laughter.

Chapter 7

WAKING UP THE next morning, Doreen hopped out of bed and was soon downstairs, with a cup of coffee in hand, sitting down at her laptop. She was determined to sort out what had happened with that trucking accident. If people needed mistletoe around here, surely there would be other sources to get it. She noted some shipping issues, and things were not coming due to highway transport on wintry roads. That could affect planes as well. With bad weather, sometimes people had to do without for a while.

Still, the truck had been on its way to Kelowna, but all its goods had been stolen or frozen, which was really too bad. Although she wasn't so sure that mistletoe could freeze. Could it? A quick internet search confirmed that frozen mistletoe was damaged, and its blossoms would soon fall off. Even if frozen and then thawed, the branches themselves would stay firm and strong, but the rest of it could get pretty nasty.

Frowning at that, she made a few phone calls. It didn't take long to confirm that the local florists were all out of any mistletoe and had no hopes of deliveries before Christmas. Just as she was pondering what else she could do, Nan called her. "I can't find mistletoe anywhere," she told her grandmother fretfully. "Between the accident last week and now with the highways closed due to the bad weather, it will quite likely be in short supply."

"Not just *quite likely*, it definitely will be," Nan snapped, and then she sighed. "It's not your fault, child. I just really wanted it for Christmas."

"What about fake mistletoe?" A shocked silence came from the other end. "Okay, so not fake then."

"No, not fake," Nan declared. "However, you're right, child. … There must be some other alternatives."

"Did you check out of town to see if anyone had any?" Doreen asked.

"No, I haven't, but are you prepared to make a trip on these roads to go get it, if I found some?"

"No, not really," Doreen confessed. "If the roads were fine, then sure. Yet, if the roads aren't any good, … you and I both know I shouldn't be out and about driving any more than you should be."

"Okay," Nan replied. "Let me put on my thinking cap and see what I can come up with." She ended the call soon after that.

Doreen wondered just what *thinking cap* her grandmother had. Yet Doreen didn't have time to worry about it, as she was curious as to what had caused the trucking accident in the first place. She quickly phoned Mack, and, when he answered, sounding distracted, she asked, "So, was that semi-truck accident with the mistletoe and all the greenery an accident, due to bad road conditions?"

"No, it wasn't an accident," he replied, with a heavy sigh. "We're waiting for forensics, and they're taking their time with lots of people away on holiday."

She thought about that. "That's not very good, but, if you're talking about the accident not being an accident, was it driver error, or did he have a heart attack, or was he poisoned or something? Or maybe the truck had some mechanical failure which caused the accident, or was it something else entirely?"

"Something else entirely," he replied, "and remember that you're not allowed on this case."

"I know, but you can't fault a gal for being curious."

"Maybe not, but that curiosity of yours tends to go in the wrong direction."

She snorted at that. "Apparently there's no wrong direction when it comes to this stuff. You should know that by now."

"There absolutely is a wrong direction where you are concerned, so don't you worry about it. We'll handle it."

"I know, but what a terrible time of the year for a family to lose somebody."

"Yes, it absolutely is. The good news in this case, if there is anything good, is he appeared to be single."

"Sure, but he has to have a mom, a dad, or somebody somewhere."

"Maybe, but we haven't found next of kin yet. Therefore, we haven't released the name of the deceased."

"Oh, that's even worse. How sad."

"It can happen, more often than not it seems."

Doreen groaned. "Nan's still fretting because there's no mistletoe. I don't understand why. It's not as if Christmas or her party will be canceled due to lack of mistletoe. And, if it is for her personal use, I don't even want to hear about it."

He snorted. "Nan will just have to deal with it. I have much bigger problems to worry about than a mistletoe shortage."

"I know, but she's asked me to get on it."

"In that case," he replied, with a smile in his tone, "you better get on it."

"You make it sound so easy."

"But for you, who has solved so many cold cases," he noted, with a chuckle, "the case of missing mistletoe surely can't be that big of a deal." And, with that, he ended the call.

She frowned at her phone, but, in a way, it was a good thing. He put Nan's request into the light of a case, and, if nothing else, that was an angle she could work with. It made her smile to even think that something could be fun about the missing mistletoe. Talk about a caper. She laughed out loud at that. Maybe not a caper, but at least something she could focus on, and she would take almost anything right now.

But first she had to deal with Mugs, who was barking to be let out into the backyard. He was the spokesman for the cat and the bird this time. She grabbed a heavy coat and joined all her animals, as they puttered around her garden, sniffing at everything. With it so cold outside, they were all soon back inside, warming up again.

Back to the mistletoe shortage issue, Doreen pondered what to do about it as she wandered through her two-story home, which was Nan's former home, in which were tons of things left behind as a result of downsizing to fit her most important items into her small apartment at Rosemoor. Nan had deliberately left behind expensive antiques as part of her household bequest to her granddaughter. Doreen had auctioned off all the antiques, which included furniture, artwork, and books. In that process, Doreen had also gone through the other things left behind, including Nan's clothing, kitchenware, even paperwork, especially when looking for the provenance regarding some of the items.

Yet Doreen didn't remember running across any Christmas decorations at all, including a full search of the basement as well. She didn't find any Valentine's Day or Halloween stuff either. Maybe Nan didn't go to the trouble decorating just for herself, but now, with Doreen here, Nan was going all out. Shaking her head, Doreen didn't understand this year's focus on Christmas, yet didn't want to disappoint Nan either. At least Doreen didn't have a cold case right now, or she really would have begrudged frittering away her time looking for some nonexistent mistletoe.

She wondered just what she could do, about finding some live mistletoe. Nan was adamant that they needed mistletoe for the Rosemoor party, and Nan couldn't possibly do without it. While Doreen wasn't particularly bothered by this, Nan apparently was horrified at the concept. Doreen sighed, deciding to dig in, anything to keep Nan happy.

Yet she kept going back to Mack's current case. He refused to discuss the fatal vehicular accident that helped to cause this mistletoe shortage. Mack couldn't release the name of the victim because next of kin hadn't been notified and wouldn't tell her what had caused the accident. Doreen understood the truck driver died, and she knew which trucking company had been involved, so maybe the employer had some information. She went onto their website, and, while it was lacking in detailed information as to the recent accident, Doreen found the staff listing.

As she reviewed the employee list, she didn't know how up to date this online list was, plus any seasonal workers weren't listed as such. Her heart went out to the driver's family, knowing that finding out via a proper notice would be so sad and heartbreaking. Yet finding out on the news prior to any private notification would be horrifying.

Doreen sighed and called the company to get further information. When she reached the receptionist, Doreen blindly pulled one of the employee names off the website listing and began, "I heard about Edgar's accident."

"Sorry," the woman said, "I think you meant Brandon."

"Oh, my goodness, I'm so sorry," Doreen replied, her tone taking a slightly higher octave. "I was reading the wrong name here."

"No, that's okay. We're all pretty shocked. It's one thing to have an accident, and we have great truckers here with excellent safe driving records, but to think that he was shot while driving, that's something we're all still adjusting to."

"Of course," Doreen murmured, struggling to hear about that herself. "Is there anything at all we can do for his family?"

"He doesn't have family," the woman replied.

"Oh my, that's all the sadder."

"It is, isn't it?" she murmured. "I mean, we've talked a lot. He's worked for us for a good ten years or more. He was just set to retire at the end of this year. Poor Brandon. He had a new adventure he was all excited about, and somehow that makes it worse," the woman muttered. "I mean, just when you've decided you are ready to go off and do something different, you don't want it all to come crashing down around you before you even get a chance to start."

"Did he say what it was? Maybe we could write his eulogy to that effect, to honor his memory."

"Something to do with importing and exporting, and he would start doing a few trips across the border. Not many, just enough to keep himself from going stir-crazy."

"Right. I guess crossing the border is a normal trip for these guys."

"We don't do any of the cross-border deliveries," the receptionist stated, "but he had some personal history with it. He wanted to start going back and forth with some friends again."

"It's nice to think he had friends. It's bad enough to think he had no family, and nobody for him at Christmas-time."

"No family left," she repeated.

"Any idea on who these friends are who he was going into business with?" Doreen asked curiously.

"Give me a moment. … I think he mentioned Jimmy."

"If you know Brandon, then maybe you know Jimmy too," Doreen noted curiously.

"I know a couple Jimmys, but I'm not sure about this one. But then again …"

"Is he the one who's … really tall and skinny?" Doreen guessed.

"No, the short one. As if maybe five foot four or so, and he comes by every once in a while. He used to work for us a while back but then left. He's always been friendly, flirty. He's not terribly attractive, but he's got that charming personality. Oh now I remember. His name is Jimmy Cooper."

"Most of the guys with that kind of personality tend to do very well regardless."

"Right, he's friendly. Too many guys think women want all this other stuff, but really they just want somebody who'll treat them well."

"Oh, I'm right there with you, sister," Doreen agreed, with a bright smile. "I think that's what's missing in so many relationships. People just want to know that somebody cares."

"Exactly," she confirmed. Doreen heard another phone line buzzing in the background, and the receptionist said, "Oops, I've got to go."

"That's all right. Thank you for your time, hon," Doreen called out cheerfully, but she already had warning lights going off in her brain.

As soon as she got off the phone, she wondered if she should call Mack. A little research on Brandon allowed her to find an acquaintance, Jimmy Cooper. She needed to talk to Mack. He might get quite angry over it all, yet she had to consider whether this info would help their investigation or hurt it. She didn't even get a chance to call him when her phone rang.

"Hey," Mack greeted her, but his tone was distracted. "I have to go to Rosemoor. Will you be there yourself anytime soon?"

"I told Nan that I would be there to help her later this afternoon. Right now I'm working on my new case."

Immediately his tone sharpened. "What new case?" he asked.

Sure enough, worry filled his tone. She snorted. "You're the one who gave me the idea."

"God help me," he muttered. "What are you talking about?"

"The case of the missing mistletoe."

After some dead silence, he laughed. "Okay, fine. You work on that."

"By the way, you know that driver of yours who was shot?"

Another silence came. "What about him?"

"I just had a talk with the trucking company's receptionist. It was apparently his last run, and he would go into business with a friend of his, maybe Jimmy Cooper, to export and import across the border. Jimmy is a short guy, really friendly, not necessarily terribly attractive but a charmer. The receptionist mentioned how Jimmy used to work there, and he was always friendly or a little flirty at times."

With a big sigh, Mack replied, "I talked to the trucking company's crew. What did you do?"

He knew her so well. "I just phoned to see if there was anything I could do for the family. The receptionist told me that he had no family and that it was such a shame, since he was just about to retire from the company and to start a new endeavor."

"I see," he noted, his tone neutral. "So, what has this got to do with mistletoe?"

"He was driving the semi-truck with the mistletoe," she stated. "So, if we've got missing mistletoe, I had to follow the source. You know, to figure out why the mistletoe is missing."

"Oh, good Lord." He gave a hard groan.

"Are you okay?" she asked, a smile in her tone.

"You'll be the death of me," he muttered.

"I hope not," she declared. "I would hate to think that being around me would lead to more stress for you."

"Yeah, it would," he snapped. "Stay out of my case."

"Absolutely I'll stay out of your case," she replied in complete and utter innocence. "Though, in all honesty, I think it would be better if we worked together on this one."

He snorted. "I mean it, Doreen. Stay out of it, please."

"I just gave you some information that I thought might

help."

"I would have gotten there on my own," he said.

"Now you know you can talk to the receptionist and can ask her those kinds of questions and get more information about it. Have a nice day." And, with that, she quickly ended the call.

Chapter 8

DOREEN WALKED TOWARD Nan's to help her out this afternoon. They were setting out some decorations all around the place. She didn't really understand what it would look like once done, but, since the project was close to Nan's heart, Doreen would do whatever she could to keep her grandmother happy.

Doreen was told by one of the residents to go to the big auditorium area of Rosemoor, which was surprisingly large. Finding Nan there, Doreen said, "I understand you're making a big deal out of this. I heard even Wendy was invited."

"Of course she is. You've done a lot for her too."

"Hardly, all I did was take her some clothing to sell."

Nan laughed. "If that was all it was, it wouldn't be much. You're right," she agreed. "Yet you forget that she got into some trouble herself, and you were the one who was there to help her out."

"Oh, yes." Doreen frowned, staring at Nan. "I completely forgot about that part."

Nan smiled. "I know, but other people have not forgotten."

Doreen grimaced. "I really don't need people thanking me for doing the right thing."

"The good news is, we'll set up this party, and hopefully everything will go smoothly, and nobody will even need to say anything more."

"Actually I like that idea," Doreen said, with a smile. "I don't really need thanks, … you know?"

"I know. That's one of the nice things about you."

"If you say so," she muttered. "Now, where do you want me to hang these decorations?"

Nan pointed to one wall. "Start over there. That wall is basically blank."

Doreen nodded. "Oh, by the way, do you happen to know a guy named Jimmy Cooper?" Nan frowned. "A short guy, friendly, a ladies' man?"

Richie walked over and glared. "Not somebody you want anything to do with," he stated, with a headshake. "You make darn sure you don't let him get into your pants."

Doreen stared at him in horror. "I was just asking because he's a friend of the man who died in the trucking incident."

"Oh, my," Richie muttered, yet he still stared at her.

"Are you getting yourself in Mack's current case?" Nan asked worriedly.

Doreen rolled her eyes. "No, of course I'm not getting into Mack's case. He wouldn't let me anyway, and you know how I feel about crossing those boundaries."

"You would cross them in a heartbeat if you thought you could get away with it," Richie declared, glaring at her but with a twinkle in his eyes.

"Maybe," Doreen admitted, "but so would you."

He let out a large guffaw and nodded. "You're right. I

probably would. On the other hand, we don't want to be pissing off poor Mack, not right now."

"Why not right now?" Doreen asked.

"He's got a case, doesn't he?" Nan asked, nudging Richie. "You know how protective he's always been about his cases."

"Yeah, and, if he's working a case," Richie added, with a shrug, though to Doreen it looked a bit off, "you should definitely stay out of it."

"*Right,*" she muttered, wondering just what the devil was going on with these two. "Whatever. I was thinking about contacting him—Jimmy Cooper."

"He's bad news," Richie repeated.

"When you say, *bad news,* do you mean *really* bad news or just *regular* bad news?"

"*Bad news,* bad news," he stated. "The worst kind. How many ways are there to say it?"

"Just checking," Doreen replied, trying to keep the conversation light. "It has to do with how you say it, the inflection, you know? There's bad news, and then there's bad news, and then—"

"Enough," Richie interrupted, holding up a hand. "He's bad news because he's a ladies' man and has a reputation of hitting on anything that moves. Plus, he gets into all kinds of trouble. Last I heard, he was involved in some questionable cross-border shenanigans."

"Cross-border, as in getting things across?" Doreen asked, trying to figure out exactly what that meant.

"I don't know exactly what he's been up to," Richie clarified, "but I've heard it's in the realm of picking up cigarettes and bringing them across the border, without declaring them. That kind of thing."

"Ah, so … smuggling basically."

"I don't know that the cops would call it smuggling. A lot of people play the border game and don't consider it illegal."

"Unless they're caught."

"Most of them don't get caught because they don't do it in a big way that would attract attention."

"Of course not," Doreen noted. "That would be breaking the law, right?"

"Exactly, and these guys don't necessarily want to break the law. They're just having fun with it."

"Is that what you think Jimmy was doing?"

"I don't know. He's not the type I shoot the breeze with to find out, you know?" When Doreen stared at him, he added, "I don't know what else to say about it. Just to advise you to stay away from him."

"I wasn't planning on going out for coffee with him," she replied.

"Good," he declared, clearly alarmed at the thought. "That would not be wise. He could be downright dangerous."

"Dangerous?" Doreen asked. "Hang on a minute. How did we get from a bad news ladies' man to dangerous so quickly?"

"Doesn't matter," Richie added. "Doreen, you don't want to muck up anything right now."

"What are you talking about?" she asked, her hands on her hips.

Suddenly looking as if he had to go somewhere, Richie said, "I'll be right back." Then he quickly disappeared.

Doreen turned to Nan and asked, "What the devil is going on?"

Nan just smiled and pointed to her ear, spinning circles with her finger, and noted, "That's just Richie."

"Oh, come on, Nan," Doreen said. "It's not as if he's all of a sudden gone loco."

"Nothing sudden about it," Nan stated cheerfully and then chuckled. "He would probably laugh at me for saying it too. Despite the occasional evidence to the contrary, he does have all his marbles right now, which is good, since we need them."

"I don't know what the devil is going on around here." Doreen stared at her grandmother. "However, you guys are making me very suspicious."

"Which, of course, is always the problem with you," Nan noted, with a big smile. "You're naturally suspicious, but I can assure you, child, that you have absolutely nothing to worry about."

"Why does that statement make me even more suspicious?" she asked, glaring at her grandmother.

"Oh my, you do have a problem then, don't you?" Nan pointed out in perfect innocence.

Doreen sighed. "It makes me wonder what all is going on here at Rosemoor. … So, do you know anything about this Jimmy Cooper guy?"

"Not really," she replied, with a wave of her hand, "but I heard talk of a group of people who play the border traffic thing. I don't know that it's limited to cigarettes, maybe not." She shook her head. "I've heard that a couple guys can get you anything you want and bring it back across the line."

"And then what, you don't have to pay duty?"

"Yeah, it's really cheap."

"Sure, I get that," Doreen replied, "but is it worth getting into trouble over?"

"If you're not the one who's on the order form, does it matter?" Nan asked, with a shrug.

"In a way, yeah, it would matter," she stated, staring at her.

"Then it matters, and, if it matters to you, then you shouldn't do it," Nan declared. "You know that you can't sit here and judge everybody because they work with a different set of ethics than you do. And you have to decide which of these battles are ones that you want to get involved in."

"Have you ever done it?"

"Oh goodness no," Nan responded. "I much prefer to support local business people. But, for some, they think it is a game, with an element of *sticking it to the man*, if you will. You know, fighting back against Big Brother or whatever."

"I don't understand all that," Doreen muttered. "Doesn't sound like such a great game to me."

"For you, it wouldn't be because you're way too serious," Nan noted. "You would get into the game and would wind up all frantic and worried that you wouldn't get out of it."

"Exactly," she agreed, "and why not? What if you got caught?"

"What if *you* got caught?" Nan asked. "These guys would just say they didn't know but would never do it again. For a first offense, they would probably get off. Easy-peasy, right?" Then she laughed.

"But that's hardly worth killing anybody over."

She turned and frowned at Doreen. "Was somebody killed over this?"

The gleam in Nan's gaze made Doreen realize just how invested they'd all become with her cases. "No, I don't think so," she muttered, with a nonchalance that fooled no one.

Nan hopped closer. "Was the semi-truck driver murdered?" she asked in low tones.

"I'm not saying a thing. Remember that this is Mack's case," Doreen replied, throwing her grandmother's words right back at her.

Nan glared at her. "Oh, now that's hardly fair."

"I know full well," Doreen stated, with a smug smile. "That's exactly what you do to me though."

"Maybe, but I could always just tell Mack that you're interfering in his case. That would put you in a pickle."

"You could," Doreen conceded, "but you should have proof."

"You're asking questions about Brandon and now this Jimmy Cooper guy," Nan stated in a crafty tone.

Doreen gasped. "That's blackmail."

"No, that's just family. We do have a reputation to uphold, now don't we?"

Doreen had no comeback for that. What could she say? Realizing her grandmother probably knew more about this Jimmy than she'd alluded to, Doreen decided to see how far she could get. "I wonder where I would find Jimmy."

"He hangs around over in Glenmore, last I heard," Nan shared a little too quickly. "There used to be a number you could call if you wanted something, but it's been a while since I touched base." Then she laughed. "However, I happened across his number in my pocket not long ago."

"For somebody who didn't ever do this, you sure know an awful lot about the process."

"I'm ancient, child. I know a lot about many things. And, while I may not have used his services, … you never know when you just might need something."

"Something?"

"Sure, anything," she said, with a shrug. "I mean, it's

just for a lark, after all."

"Please, no more larks." Doreen stared at her grandmother. "It's not just us who would have problems here, but right now it could really reflect badly on Mack."

At that, Nan stopped and frowned. "Oh, yeah."

"So, you do remember Jimmy?"

"Yeah, of course I remember him," she stated crossly, "but honestly, I hadn't really considered it from Mack's point of view."

"It's a whole new world now," Doreen pointed out. "We've gotten involved in an awful lot of cases, and, from Mack's perspective, he's held to a higher standard, and, as such, we are too."

"That seems terribly boring," Nan muttered, staring at Doreen.

"It might be boring," she conceded, "but it doesn't have to be."

"Oh, of course it does, when we are talking about the cops. Still, we can probably find another way to liven up our investigations." Then Nan sighed. "I really don't want to think that any of us prefers to be *boring*."

"Of course not," Doreen replied, "but it is the truth when it comes to how Mack would see these things."

"It is *kind of* the truth," Nan conceded, with a sigh. "I'll have to put some thought into that. Anyway you really shouldn't go down there on your own."

"It's Glenmore, so not very far away, and it's hardly *down there*. It's not in any of the bad areas. After all Glenmore is known to be for families, for crying out loud, so it's hardly a problem."

"Maybe not a problem," Nan noted, "but it's still not a place I would have you go alone."

Doreen sighed. "Nan, what are you not telling me?"

"It's just that this Jimmy, he's a bit of a lothario …" she shared, "and women do tend to fall all over him."

"Do you really think I'll be falling all over him?" she asked her grandmother.

"Oh, no, dear, not you, not when you've got Mack."

Doreen stared at Nan. "Good Lord, so what's the issue?"

"I'm not really sure," Nan muttered, as she stared off in the distance. "I guess I just would feel … better somehow if you didn't go."

"You might feel better, but that's not an answer."

"Of course it's an answer. I just would feel better if you didn't go. How is that *not* an answer?"

Doreen shook her head. "Look. If I go, I'll only talk to this guy."

"Of course, of course," Nan muttered, but she kept frowning.

"You can't really think that I would be swayed by this guy?"

Nan shrugged. "He's got quite a track record. … Women I wouldn't have expected to fell heavily for him."

"Oh, man," Doreen muttered. "Now you're really making me want to go see this guy."

"No, no, no, don't. Don't even think that," she cried out in alarm. "You shouldn't do this. Definitely not now."

"But this is part of my investigation of the case. So I do need to get a hold of him."

Nan reached into her pocket and pulled out the slip of paper. As she looked down at the number in her hand and, with her own phone in her other hand, she called him. Sure enough, the voice on the other end boomed in delight. "Nan, how are you?"

Chapter 9

SHOCKED AT HER grandmother's impromptu actions, Doreen stepped up, her hands on her hips, and glared at Nan.

"I'm doing just fine, Jimmy," Nan replied cheerfully. "I heard that a friend of yours died."

"Oh my gosh, he sure did. I'm just beside myself over it. You know that we just set up a business and all." He sounded sorrowful. "Man, I don't even know what to do now."

"What business?" Nan asked.

"You know," he quipped, with a chuckle.

"So, same old, same old?"

"Yeah, same old, same old."

"So why set up as a business now?" Nan asked, with that lively curiosity of hers that seemed to let her get away with asking questions from anybody, and they all just volunteered the answers.

"Ah, well, … he wanted to do a little bit more of it, you know, so he could work less at his day job."

"Working smarter is always a good idea," Nan replied coyly.

Doreen watched her grandmother in action, and it appeared that Nan could be quite the charmer herself.

"I mean, especially if it was profitable and all. Of course you don't want to get caught. I can't imagine that would go well for you."

"That was one of the things we were talking about. We don't want to get caught. We don't want any of that strife, but working nine-to-five at our age was not exactly what we wanted to do either."

"No, no, of course not. I was really sad to hear about Brandon."

"Oh, and the fact that he was shot too," Jimmy added, with a sad tone. "It … just breaks my heart."

"Does he have any family? Is there anyone we should do something for?"

"No, no family," he muttered. "He was all alone. Maybe that's why it's hitting me so hard too. You know that's my situation as well."

"I know," Nan said. "You never did find that one lovely woman to settle down with and marry, did you?"

"No, I sure didn't. Nobody will have me."

Nan laughed. "Oh, come on. Don't you mean that you couldn't settle down to just one?"

"I won't say you're wrong there," he replied in that bright, cheerful tone. "Anyway, what are you up to? I haven't heard from you in a long time."

"Oh, I just thought I would call and pay my respects for your buddy," she shared. "Of course, my dearly beloved granddaughter is wondering if there was anything untoward about his death, but, if he was shot, there apparently was."

"Oh, my goodness. She's that private eye person, isn't she?"

"Not formally," Nan replied in a cagey tone.

"That just gave me a thought though. Do you think she would give me a hand to sort it all out?"

Nan looked over at Doreen, who was shaking her head at a crazy rate. Nan frowned and glared at her.

Doreen leaned forward and interjected, "Hey, Jimmy. This is Doreen. I can't do anything or get involved in an active case."

"Oh, right. I think I heard something about that. The police don't like it, do they?"

"No, they certainly don't."

"You know that Brandon ended up doing time a few years back."

"Really?" Doreen asked, her ears perking up at that news.

"It was an open-and-shut deal, B&Es, but he didn't do it."

"What do you mean, he didn't do it?"

"He was doing B&Es back then but not with me. And he swears he didn't do one of those B&Es. So, you know, *that's* a cold case."

"It depends on whether it's on the books as a cold case though, which it wouldn't be, not if he did time. If he wasn't guilty though, did he say something or at least try to mount a defense?"

"He did, but he was afraid to push it too far because whoever had really done it would come back after him."

"Interesting," she murmured.

"After he got out of jail, he tried to get the freedom people to look at it, but nobody would."

"That's interesting too. I can always talk to Mack and see if that qualifies as letting me in on the current case."

"It would be great if you could," Jimmy said eagerly. "Considering Brandon was shot, and there didn't appear to be any reason for it, I'm a little worried about what might happen the next time I go out."

"I guess it depends on whether your smuggling operation involves any B&E operations. Maybe somebody doesn't like the smuggling part."

"And yet, what's not to like?" Jimmy asked. "We've been doing this for a long time, and nobody's really cared so far."

"Outside of the police, you mean," she noted in a wry tone.

"Well, yeah, them," Jimmy conceded, "but it's not as if we're heavy into crime or anything."

She shook her head as she realized just how much these people thought of it as a game and not criminal activity. She knew that Mack would have a completely different viewpoint on it.

"Hey, why don't you come down and talk to me more about it?" he suggested, his tone lightening. "It's lonely down here, and it is Christmastime."

"That depends on if you've got any information on what happened to Brandon back then with the B&E."

"Oh, I can dredge up his old files," Jimmy noted. "I lived with the guy after all, so all that stuff is right here."

"Have the police been to your place?"

"Sure. They went to his new place too. He had recently moved out. That was in the last month or so, but, up until then, we shared a house."

"Why did he move out?" Doreen asked.

"Ah, you know how it is. I think he had thoughts that maybe he would get himself a girlfriend. He may have felt I was cramping his style in a way."

"Oh, I see."

Nan nodded. "I can see that too," Nan added, "not to mention the fact that you do have a bit of a roving eye."

"I might have a bit of a roving eye," he conceded, with a laugh, "but I do understand boundaries … kind of."

Nan laughed. "You might understand boundaries, but I'm not sure you quite know how to respect them."

"I don't know about that," he countered, still with laughter in his tone. "I mean, I never tried to *take* the women."

"No, they just naturally preferred you?" Doreen asked, with a smile.

"Exactly, so why don't you come on down, and I'll show you what I've got regarding Brandon's cold case."

"Sure, I can do that," Doreen agreed. As soon as she got the address, she ended the call and looked over at Nan. "I thought you didn't want me to go see him?"

"It's probably better if you do go see him," Nan explained, "and then we won't have to worry about it."

"I don't understand how this is different," Doreen muttered, staring at her grandmother.

"What? It's just good to get it out of the way. So, if you are persuaded by this guy, then Mack needs to know that you guys really don't have what it takes."

"Good God, Nan. It's not as if meeting some guy out of the blue will change my mind about Mack," she stated in exasperation. "I'm not as fickle as that."

"No, maybe not." Nan eyed her granddaughter shrewdly. "But the question is, are you serious enough for poor Mack right now?"

"Just stop," Doreen told Nan. "Please, enough already. Do you really find me that shallow?"

"You should go see Jimmy now," Nan declared.

"Fine, I will," she muttered. "Mack won't be home anytime soon anyway. So I'll be there and back before he comes by my place."

"Good." Still, Nan frowned. "Here's a thought. Maybe I'll come with you."

Doreen stared at her. "Are you up for a field trip?"

"Absolutely, and, besides, we won't be gone long, right?"

"No, we don't have to be. You're the one who seems to think this will be a big deal."

"I don't *want* it to be a big deal," she clarified, "but sometimes we get surprised by these things."

Not sure where Nan was going with any of this, Doreen gathered together the animals. "Let me go get my car. I'll come right back, so wait for me in the parking lot, okay?"

It took no time and, as soon as she returned to Rosemoor, she opened up the passenger door for Nan, who could barely contain her excitement. "Let's go on a field trip then," Doreen announced. "It shouldn't take very long at all." And, with that, an excited Nan at her side, Doreen headed down the road toward Jimmy's address. It was about a fifteen-minute drive.

By the time they pulled up in front of the address, Nan looked up and nodded. "This is it."

Doreen turned to her grandmother and asked, "What are you not telling me?"

"Nothing," she said, blinking those baby blues at her.

"You two were involved, weren't you?" Doreen asked in disgust. "Don't tell me that you smuggled things with him too?"

"No, not really." Nan gave a dismissive wave. "Still, with all the hype, you've got to try it, right?"

"No, you don't." Doreen gave her an eye roll.

"It was a long time ago, dear." She patted Doreen's hand. "Nothing I can get caught for now."

"Says you." They got out with Goliath and Mugs securely leashed, Thaddeus on Doreen's shoulder, and walked to the front door. It opened almost immediately. Nan was snatched into a big hug, while Jimmy's gaze, bright and assessing, looked over Nan's head to check out Doreen.

She shook her head at him. "It's not good form to assess one woman, while you're hugging another one." She also noted that her animals weren't in a rush to greet this man. *Interesting.*

He burst out laughing at that, then stepped back to look at Nan. "Oh, I like her already."

"Of course you do," Nan declared, with almost a sigh of resignation in her voice. She looked at her granddaughter and added, "Come on in. This is Jameson, but he prefers Jimmy. Jimmy, this is my granddaughter, Doreen."

She smiled at him and said, "Pleased to meet you."

He looked at her quizzically. "She's definitely not what I expected. And an animal lover, I see."

To Doreen, it didn't appear that he liked her animals. That was another strike against him.

"If you'd seen pictures of her, you wouldn't have had a different expectation," Nan stated, nodding at her granddaughter to come in. "Get in here, child, and shut that door. It's cold."

"Of course." She quickly stepped inside, her animals sticking close to her. Doreen was not sure why Nan was acting the way she was. But absolutely nothing about the man in front of her would make Doreen's heart—or anybody else's—jump.

He was balding, definitely weathered, and looked as if he'd been around the booze for way too long, forgetting to leave it behind. He was also very short and at least thirty years her senior, if not forty. She hid a smile as Nan looked at him, then at Doreen, one eyebrow raised. Doreen shook her head, and, with a sigh of relief, Nan nodded.

"Of course not," Nan whispered. "You're too smart for that."

Not even sure what that meant, but knowing that something was going on here that Doreen didn't understand, she followed Nan into the living room, where Jimmy waited for them. Doreen muttered quietly to Nan, "I still don't get it."

"Interesting," Nan murmured.

As they walked through Jimmy's house, Doreen noted the antique furniture, then realized that this guy probably got big bucks from whatever he had been doing. It was the illegal part that would never go down well in her department, particularly after dealing with her ex. As she looked around, she smiled and asked, "Live alone by any chance?"

"Yes, and it's obvious, isn't it?" he replied gloomily. "All the ladies pass through my arms," he quipped, winking at Nan. "And yet I wasn't smart enough to take any of them on full-time."

Doreen's gaze went from one to the other, but her mind balked at what the wink may have meant. She shook her head, telling herself it was none of her business. Plus, she was *so* not going there, not even for a moment. She began, "So, your friend."

"Ah, yes." Jimmy pointed to a box set off to the side. "Those were all his records. Not sure it'll be of any help to you, but it's possible."

"Maybe." She nodded. "Depending on just what it is

that we think we're looking at."

"I don't know," Jimmy admitted. "I didn't have anything to do with the B&Es."

"And yet"—she turned to face him—"you both lived together and were both involved in smuggling goods across the border."

"Sure, but it was just a game. It wasn't real."

"It'll be real if the cops find out."

He moistened his lips nervously. "That wouldn't be good." His gaze went from her, to Nan, and back to her again. "I really can't have that happen."

Doreen sighed. "And what about your friend Brandon? What was this about a crime he didn't commit?"

"He got charged for multiple crimes," Jimmy explained, shrugging his shoulders, "but one of the burglaries he didn't do. And it always pissed him off that he paid the price, when somebody else had done the crime. He also believed that he knew who it was, but I can't remember just what he told me." He frowned and added, "It was a weird name, like Potter or something."

"Potter?" Doreen repeated, frowning.

"Yeah, I don't know for sure, some weird name."

"Like a nickname?"

"No, I think it was a real name," he replied. "It was one of those kinds of names that you could never really forget, but, of course, because you couldn't forget it, it was incredibly hard to remember," Jimmy explained, with a brilliant smile in her direction.

Apparently Jimmy thought that smile was supposed to make him all the more endearing to Doreen. Instead it had the opposite effect. "Okay, and who do you think would have shot Brandon in his truck?"

His smile fell away, and he shook his head. "Honest to God, I don't know."

"And has it made you rethink your business strategies?" she asked him. "Because, if it hasn't, maybe it should."

"Do you really think it has something to do with smuggling?" he asked anxiously.

"I don't know about smuggling, but maybe the B&E thing," she suggested, "especially if Brandon found the guilty party and could produce proof about the crime he served time for and maybe threatened this person in some way."

"Brandon might have done that too," Jimmy replied. "He was just foolish enough to have that much bravado."

"Bravado is one thing," Doreen noted, "but threatening somebody else with jail time, that's a whole different story, as you should well know."

He looked at her nervously. "I don't want to do any jail time."

"I get that," she replied. "So, when the police come around asking questions, you might want to be a little more honest and open about your answers."

He frowned. "But, if I do that, I can't cross the border at all anymore."

Nan patted his hand. "Then maybe it's time for that caper to end."

"Do you think so?" he asked. "I'll be awfully short on money then."

Doreen nodded. "I get that, and it's a consideration, but there are other ways to make an income without putting your life at risk."

At that, his eyes widened. Then he looked at the box and pushed it toward her. "You better take that away," he said. "I ain't got no idea what happened to Brandon, but I don't want to be the next one killed."

"Is there any reason to think you might be?" Doreen asked, not touching the box, her gaze still assessing him. "Have you done anything or gotten involved with any shady characters?"

"I don't think so," he said, "but we don't really do a customer background check when we take on these border jobs."

"Right. And you have worked at this for how long? Thirty years?" she asked, closely watching him. "Times have changed, and the cops have changed, and, most important, the competition has changed."

Once again Nan nodded and added, "It's about time for you to change too, my friend."

He looked at her, his shoulders sagging. "It'll really be tough," he pointed out. "I'm not sure I can even keep my house."

"Right," Nan agreed. "So we might need to help you find another income stream."

"Are you at a pensionable age?" Doreen asked. "That would help."

"*Sure*"—he sent her an eye roll—"but it's not as if the pension will be much."

Doreen tilted her head. "But, if you've been wise with your money over the years, and if the house is paid for, it should at least cover your living expenses."

He frowned at her, then turned to Nan. "She really just said that, didn't she?"

Nan chuckled. "Yeah, she sure did. Yet she's right. If everything was paid for, the pension would probably be enough."

"It's *not* all paid for," Jimmy admitted, as he collapsed

onto the chair beside him. He looked around at the old house and added, "Honestly, I've been thinking I might need to sell it for a while now."

"I don't know what the market is today versus tomorrow," Doreen began, "but it might not be a bad idea. Plus, with all these antiques in the house, that could make you flush again, depending on what's going on in your world. You could always look at other options, like where Nan lives."

He shook his head. "Rosemoor? I don't see myself in that place. … Nan held off until now." He turned to Doreen pointedly. "And honestly, she moved because of you, Doreen."

"I was ready," Nan claimed.

"Sure, but you wouldn't have considered it but for the fact that she needed a home," he pointed out.

Doreen stated, "I would never let Nan suffer for what she did for me."

"You're fine," Nan replied gently. "I don't need the money."

"I know you don't," Doreen said, with a smile. "And, if you did, I would expect you to tell me."

"Of course, child. I helped you, and you can help me."

But Nan's careless attitude meant that Nan would never ask for help, if it ever came down to that. "We'll deal with whatever we need to, when and if the time comes," Doreen stated.

"I won't need help. I have enough money invested to not have to worry."

"And then there's the question of whether you would actually tell me that you needed help," Doreen muttered, with a sigh.

Nan gave her a bright grin. "You know that I still have my jewelry. I have all kinds of things."

"Uh, don't even mention jewelry." Doreen sighed. "Apparently I have to deal with my ex's jewelry collection as well."

Nan's gaze lit up. "Ooh, that'll be so much fun."

Doreen shook her head. "No, it won't. The only thing I want, if it's still there—which is questionable, since he tried to force me to get rid of it—would be your grandmother's necklace."

"Oh my." Nan's hand went to her heart. "I'd forgotten about that. I gave that to you a very long time ago."

"You did, and Mathew didn't like it," she shared, with that same fatalistic tone that she used whenever it came to conversations around him. She turned herself back to the issue at hand. "So, back to business. What's this guy's name again?"

"*Hmm*, Pengo or Potter or something," Jimmy said, "but I don't know his last name."

She took out her little notepad and quickly wrote it down. Thaddeus decided to show himself and announced, "Thaddeus is here. Thaddeus is here."

"Oh my God, a bird." Jimmy almost jumped out of his seat.

Doreen explained, "Thaddeus was Nan's pet, along with the cat. Now I'm looking after them."

Jimmy nodded, as he regrouped, then pointed at her notepad. "Look at that," he declared in admiration. "You came prepared."

"That's something you don't take very long to sort out when you're doing this kind of work," Doreen explained. "These details disappear way too quickly." He looked at her and smiled. She sighed. "It's what I do and how I figured out how to do it."

"I'm happy to hear it," Jimmy replied. "Your grandmother has had a huge impact in my life, so I'm happy to see her granddaughter carrying on in her ways."

"Oh, I don't think so," Doreen said.

"Oh my, no," Nan replied.

Both Doreen and Nan spoke at the same time, and then, sharing a look, burst out laughing.

"Anyway," Doreen noted, looking back at Nan, "come on. I've got to get you back before you miss your dinner."

Nan raised her hand in a wave to Jimmy. "I used to be totally okay to miss dinner," she shared, "but now that we have a really good cook, the food is great."

"Is it?" he asked wistfully. "I'll probably open a can of spam and make a sandwich." When Nan looked at him in horror, he shrugged. "You know how it is. You make your choices, and you learn to live with them."

Doreen didn't want to get involved, but she could see Nan warming up to him. "Let's go, Nan. Remember that Jethro and Richie are waiting."

She looked over at her in confusion for a moment, then nodded. "Jethro and Richie have both taken to retirement home living just fine. You should consider it too, Jimmy." Nan waved goodbye again and followed Doreen, who had the box in her arms.

As she got the animals into the car, Nan stated, "You are very good at compartmentalizing who you help and who you don't help."

"I'm not trying to," Doreen replied, "but the last thing you need is to take on any more boyfriends. Isn't two at a time enough?"

"Jimmy and I do have a bit of a history," Nan shared, with a funny note in her tone.

"I got that," Doreen muttered. "The trouble is, you seem to have an awful lot of history with an awful lot of people." When Nan felt no shame whatsoever and just fluttered her lashes in a comical way, Doreen burst out laughing. "I get it," she said, still rolling her eyes. "You've enjoyed your life."

"I did enjoy my life, and I still do," Nan confirmed, with a smile. "You need to enjoy yours a little more."

"I'm getting there, Nan. Honest, I am."

"I know you are, child, and I don't mean to tease you"— yet she gave her granddaughter a hard look—"but I do worry."

"You don't need to worry," Doreen murmured, glancing over at her.

"You may say that, but, for me, it's a whole different story," Nan noted. "You're the only family I have, and I want to ensure that you will be okay in the future."

Chapter 10

DOREEN WOKE THE next morning, eager to get started on tracking down this Potter or Pengo person, who supposedly committed the B&E that Brandon had served time for. The fact that Brandon was now dead, shot while driving his semi, piqued her interest. She started by requesting files from the public archives. Then she thought about it for a moment and, frowning, picked up the phone and called Mack.

"What's up?" he asked, distracted.

"Can you pull Brandon's old files, please?" There was silence for a bit, and she braced herself.

"Why?" he asked cautiously.

"One, we know that he's dead, and that's very unfortunate. Two, we know he was murdered, which is even more unfortunate. Three, apparently he was spouting off about an older case—a cold case, I might add—that he served time for but still claimed he was innocent."

"Seriously?" Mack asked, with a sigh.

"Yeah, seriously." She was beaming with success at having found a way to get involved in Mack's current case.

"So, you're telling me that because Brandon opened up

some protest file, it's something you get to work on?"

She didn't say anything, just waited for him to get on with it.

"Let me look into it, and I'll get back to you." He promptly ended the call.

Not exactly the answer she was hoping for, but he didn't tell her to butt out, so that was a good thing. She had to remember that what she was doing was still technically skirting the edges of their agreement. It was an agreement she fully intended to abide if she could, but she was still okay with evading the rules somewhat.

Of course, if something was going on here that needed to be settled, she was perfectly capable of skirting issues when needed. Still, she didn't want to piss off Mack unnecessarily. She certainly didn't want that between them, so she often endured this *wait until he came around* phase, until he saw it from her side of the fence.

When he called her back a little bit later, he admitted, "You're right. He did open a file with the freedom group, asking to be exonerated and saying he was innocent of one of these charges. They refused to look at it," he shared, "because he admitted to being guilty to all the others."

"So he did serve time for the others, but he also served time for the one in question. Despite all of that, he remained adamant that he didn't do it."

"And?" he asked curiously. "What's the point of opening this if nobody is left to prove he's innocent?"

"Potentially somebody is guilty of a crime and is still walking around free," she pointed out. "I get that the whole guilty thing is less of a concern for you, but it is a concern for me."

He groaned. "Anyway, I pulled the file, and I'm sending

you the bits I can send you right now."

"You could send me all of it," she protested. "Brandon's gone, and it's not as if I can ask him for permission. I already have a box of stuff."

"What do you mean, you have a box?" His tone sharpened.

"I have a box I got from his business partner who happens to be …" She hesitated and then sighed. "God help me for saying this, and Lord knows these are words I never thought I would have to utter, but I got it from one of Nan's old flames."

"Good Lord, another one?" he exclaimed.

"Apparently she was a popular girl in her day." Doreen chuckled.

"Right," Mack muttered. "Okay, so this box, what about it?"

"Somewhere in here, according to Jimmy, is the information on the guy who really did that particular B&E."

"In that case I'll need to see it, won't I?" he asked briskly.

"Which is why I'm in the process of scanning it all in, so I can send it to you."

"Would you really send it to me?" he asked, with a note of humor.

"Of course," she declared, "But I might have held back a little bit."

"Yeah, so why am I imagining that your definition of *a little bit* could be different from mine?" he asked, with a snort.

"Oh, don't be silly. I'm almost done, and I can send this off fairly soon." She ran the last few pages through as she talked to him, hoping he would let her in on any news on the current case, but, of course, Mack being Mack, he didn't give her a thing. "Okay. All done. I'll just email this all to you." She quickly forwarded the scans to him, quite proud of the continuing improvement in her electronic skills. "I think that's it, but there could be other stuff in the box. As I go through it, I'll send you what I find."

"Do that." Then he added, "Please." And, with that, he quickly rang off.

She wondered if it was just a little bit too quickly. She wanted to call him back and ask him what he was trying to hide but figured that wouldn't get her very far. Soon afterward, she poured herself a cup of coffee, and went outside to enjoy the view. It was a good day, or so she hoped it would be. Then Nan called her.

"What'd you find?" she asked.

"Nothing yet," Doreen replied. "I'm still going through the box. I scanned in a bunch of stuff and sent it off to Mack."

"Oh, yes, of course," Nan noted, with that air of knowledge. "We have to keep Mack in the loop, don't we?"

"If we want to keep interfering in his cases, then yes," Doreen stated, "or we're not likely to get far."

"It's not that we want to keep interfering," Nan pointed out brightly, "but more about moving on this."

Doreen sighed. "I'm not sure everybody would agree with you."

"Of course not," Nan muttered. "I think I'll try to get him into the home here."

"Who?"

"Jimmy, of course. Remember we talked to him about it briefly."

"Right," she muttered, remembering the way Nan was

around him, "And you think he would be happier there, or will he raise Cain?"

After a moment's pause Nan replied, "He'll undoubtedly do both, but I think it's still better for him."

"It may well be better for him, just as long as you're aware of the potential consequences."

"Yep, though that's not my problem," she declared, with a cheeky tone.

"If you say so." Doreen almost groaned out loud at the thought of the lothario everybody seemed to be so worried about taking on all the women in the retirement home.

"He doesn't need to be lonely, and plenty of people are here for him to socialize with," Nan stated.

"I can't argue with that, Nan. I suggest you try calling him to see if he's even interested in Rosemoor."

"I already have, and he's coming to take a look. He admits it's only because I say the food is so good that he's even contemplating it. He's had a thing about avoiding a retirement home all these years."

"I certainly agree that—for some people, at a certain point in their lives—it seems to be a very good option."

"Exactly, and I think that would apply in his case as well."

"If you say so," Doreen muttered.

"I'll leave you to your work now. I'll wait for him out front, as he's already on his way."

"Already?" she asked in astonishment.

"Yep, … already. Absolutely no point in waiting when you're our age."

Something about the way she said that made Doreen's eyes widen. "You're not talking …"

"Never mind," Nan cut her off. "I won't bore you with

details." Then she quickly ended the call.

"Good Lord, Nan. Whoever would have thought you would be such a trial at this stage of your life?" Doreen muttered, as she stared off in the distance.

Who would have thought that life in an old folk's home could be so filled with all these clandestine activities? Yet they all seemed to be perfectly happy and healthy, moving forward in whatever way they wanted. It was hard to argue with any of that, especially considering the reality that Nan was often at the leading edge of the trouble down there. As long as she could continue to be good and to stay out everybody's way, Doreen shouldn't have any more problems at Rosemoor to deal with. But, with Nan, that was never an easy thing to do.

Chapter 11

I T TOOK A bit, but eventually Doreen found a number for the Freedom Project, and, armed with the information she had so far, she contacted them to find out why Brandon's request had been turned down.

When the lady on the other end, Lucy, realized that Doreen had no legal right to ask all these questions, Lucy wasn't very forthcoming. Doreen pressed her a bit. "But the fact of the matter is, your project is here and is not necessarily just for people who are lawyers," Doreen argued. "You're here for anybody who has been unjustly treated. Is that not correct?"

"Yes, of course it is," Lucy agreed. "However, we're also very short on time and man-hours, so we must put our energy into the cases we have a good chance of winning. I won't say any more about that."

"Ah, so not necessarily the cases you believe or don't believe in but the ones that have the best chance of surviving the legal system."

"Something like that, yes. Also we understand that Brandon is now deceased."

"Yes, that's quite correct. I just wondered how far any of

his requests went."

"It didn't go anywhere," Lucy stated firmly. "We looked into his request, and it might have been something we could have dealt with, but he was admittedly guilty of plenty, which doesn't help his case. And now, seeing that Brandon is no longer with us, it's definitely not something we have any interest in pursuing."

"Just like that?"

"Not out of callousness," she said sharply, "and I know it may sound insensitive, but it's simply a matter of a lack of time and energy."

"Of course. I do understand that."

"It would be nice if more people did," Lucy said ruefully, "because honestly, a lot of people hold those decisions against us. They have zero understanding of the investment we make in these cases. Now, if we had the money, we could and would do so much more. Yet we just don't have those kinds of resources."

"So, it really comes down to a funding issue?"

"Yes," she declared. "It's definitely a money issue. Like everyone else, we must live within our means, and that comes down to limited manpower, which limits the cases we can take on. So, any time you want to donate, feel free."

As Doreen ended the call, she stared out at the world around her, realizing she may well have money that could be put to good use and donated to the Freedom Project. But how did she figure out how to do it, without messing it up, spending it all and losing the financial security it appeared she would have? Again she was reminded that she should speak to Nick and Bernard about these financial issues. She added it to her notepad to remind her to deal with this later.

She tossed that into the back of her mind, as her phone

was buzzing. It was Mack's brother.

"Hey," Nick greeted her. "I tried calling earlier, but the line was busy for a while."

"Yep, a busy day," she said.

"I've never quite understood that," he muttered. "How is it that you are always so busy?"

"You would be surprised," she muttered.

"Who were you calling this time?" he asked curiously.

"The Freedom Project. … You know? The people who help those who have been incarcerated wrongly to get out of jail."

After a moment of silence, Nick asked, "Are you on another case?"

"Kind of. Maybe, maybe not. I'm just bored."

"Bored?" he asked in astonishment.

"Yes, … bored. And that apparently is something nobody else really understands."

"I can understand it in theory," he replied. "Still, it's not something I typically have any experience with, though."

"Meaning, you're never bored?"

"Meaning, I've never really had a chance to get bored. Being a lawyer, there's always so much work to do. We do live in a litigious world." He chuckled. "So, boredom is not something I get to experience with my schedule. Lots of other things, but never boredom."

"And I suppose that's fair," she muttered. "I mean, it's not as if any of us get a chance to do things the way we want."

"*Uh-oh*. Sounds as if you're heading off on a crusade again."

"No, no, I'm not. … Well, maybe I am."

And he burst out laughing. "Does Mack know?"

"Maybe." Then she added, "Speaking of Mack. Remember those watch collections we were talking about? You know, that Mathew had?"

"Yeah?"

"Do you think Mack would like a new watch for Christmas? If I could get one out of Mathew's collection?"

Nick paused. "I know Mack would love a new watch for Christmas. He's mentioned a couple times that he needs to get a new watch."

"Right," she agreed. "The thing is, I don't know if one of Mathew's watches would do. Mathew didn't wear them very much. Plus, it would be Mathew's watch, and maybe that's a big no-no for Mack."

"What kind of watches were they?"

"I don't really know, but I do remember when he bought one of them. He spent an outrageous amount of money on it, but he was really happy with it."

"What do you consider an outrageous amount of money? I mean, you've called *a grand* outrageous many times since we met."

"I'm thinking he paid $175,000 for this one watch," she muttered.

There was dead silence on the other end. "Doreen, we really need to get a full accounting of everything in his place, like today. Are you sure you don't want to fly down there and go through everything? I'm thinking now that maybe I need to go in person as well."

"Only if you think we need to," she replied. "I mean, I don't really know whether that's a lot of money for a watch or not. I did a quick search on Google, and they go from about twenty bucks on eBay to hundreds of thousands of dollars."

"Exactly," Nick replied. "Yet I can tell you that, when Mack's talking about a watch, he's talking about a watch he could actually wear."

"And why wouldn't he wear one of Mathew's?" she asked, frowning. "What's the point of spending that kind of money if it's not even a watch you can wear?"

He laughed. "You certainly could wear it," he declared.

She was more confused now. "But that's what I'm asking about," she said in exasperation. "Why is everything so overly complicated?"

"It's not intended to be complicated." He chuckled. "Just some things get a little more complicated than you expect."

She stared down at her phone. "Meaning, *I* make it more complicated, is that what you're saying?"

He burst out laughing. "No, I don't even want to say that. What I am saying is that sometimes you have rings that you can wear anywhere, and then you have the ones that are so valuable that you don't want to wear them in case it might get damaged or stolen."

"Oh." And the thought continued to ring in her mind. "So, you think those watches from my ex will be too valuable to wear? Which means, that's not a normal price for a watch, is that what you're saying?"

"Yeah, that's exactly what I'm saying," he stated. "I'm not saying that Mack wouldn't like it, but it won't be something he would use daily without having to worry about it."

"No point having a watch if he won't wear it. I just want him to have something he would like and use."

"Then why don't you go for something that is still a good watch, but is a whole lot less money?" He mentioned a few brands that she didn't recognize.

"Hang on. Let me write those down. And does anybody in town sell these?"

"Sure, and that's a good idea. If you get it from somebody local, you can get a warranty and hopefully trust them to look after the watch and to keep it in good running condition."

"Right, so maybe I'll go to the jewelers."

"Don't you know a couple in town?"

"I do know a couple. I'm just not sure they'll be happy to see me."

A choked-off laugh came first. "You know that issues like these always arise when you tend to put people behind bars, right?"

"I do know somebody who could help me. Remember the guy who evaluated your mother's jewels?"

"Right, so, in essence, you do have somebody you can talk to. Just confirm you get Mack a watch he can wear on a daily basis."

"Versus?" she asked in confusion.

"Versus a watch he would take out and admire every once in a while but would never wear."

"But that would be useless," she cried out.

"Exactly, and that's what I'm saying. Get something useful. That would suit Mack a whole lot more."

Chapter 12

*G*ET SOMETHING USEFUL? The words rolled around in the back of her mind, until she figured out a way forward. Now with her phone calls done, she started researching good working-man watches. That made her feel so much better when she realized the price was something commensurate with a working man's wage. She thought that Mack might like a fancier watch, yet she was afraid it might bring up something she hadn't even considered—which was now the vast difference in money they each had, or she would have when it all came home to roost.

She wasn't even sure when that would happen. Yet it did seem like eventually it would happen, and, therefore, it might be something that would cause Mack to second guess having a relationship with her. That wouldn't make her happy at all. That made her sound as if lots of things in life didn't make her happy, and she didn't mean that. She really didn't. There were so many good things about her world these days. And the money didn't matter, but having experienced not having any, as compared to having some, she didn't want to be without again if she didn't have to be. She knew Mack would agree totally. So the last thing she wanted to do would be to get him a gift that would highlight what he didn't have.

Wondering just what she was supposed to do about that, she contacted the jeweler in town, the one she'd had the occasion to work with, and asked if they had any good working-man's watches.

With a note of humor in his tone, he replied, "Sure, Doreen. Come on down and let's take a look and see what you call a working-man's watch."

She winced, sensing a pitfall coming ahead of her. "I just mean a watch that Mack would wear daily," she explained, "and not one that he would feel as if he couldn't put on his wrist."

"Right." She heard the humor in his tone. "We have a huge selection of watches, so come on down and take a look. Let's see what Mack would like."

"How do you know that though? Have you taken a look at the watch he has?"

"Yeah, the band has been repaired multiple times, and he told me that there's no point in doing much more than that because it will just keep getting ruined because of his job, and that's a really good point. We need something that he can put on and wear every day and not worry if it gets banged up or scraped up somehow."

"Or torn off because of snagging it on a fence or something," she added. "I mean, he works really hard and may well be hard on his watch, but he still needs to know that he's on time or not."

"Right."

And again she heard the amusement in the jeweler's tone. "I sound silly over this, don't I?" she asked. "I've got to tell you that I've never really had Christmas, and I don't really know what I'm supposed to do about it, but I get the impression that I'm supposed to do something."

"It's really more about doing something because you *want* to do something," he said gently.

"I want to do something, but I don't know how one decides what that something is," she muttered.

"I suggest you come down, and we'll take a look. We'll see if you like the look of something that you think Mack would enjoy. Besides, you can bring the animals with you. We haven't seen them in a while."

"Oh." She looked down at Mugs, who was slumped at her feet. "That sounds wonderful."

"Then come on. I'll put on the teakettle." And, with that, he ended the call.

She groaned as she looked down at her animals. "Apparently everybody seems to think I do nothing but drink tea."

It wasn't that she did nothing but drink tea, but more so that everybody else seemed to drink tea and assumed she would as well. But there was no time like the present, and she needed to sort out Mack's gift early, so she would quit worrying about it.

She quickly packed up the animals and drove down to the jewelry store. As she walked in, Thaddeus immediately flapped his wings and cooed, "Thaddeus is here. Thaddeus is here."

The jeweler—his name was Danny—walked over to say hi. "Hey, Thaddeus. I haven't seen you in a while, buddy."

Thaddeus chuckled. "*He, he, he, he,*" and that went on several more times, making Danny laugh.

When they were finally done greeting each other, he looked over at Doreen. "Okay, so you're thinking about getting Mack a new watch for Christmas."

"I was thinking it might be a gift that he could use," she clarified, a little unsure of what to expect here. "He has a very practical spirit, and he's not really into unnecessary expenses. Yet I don't know that he's ever had a fancy watch either."

"Maybe for the moment, let's just focus on something that you think he would like that's practical. It's easy enough to step it up on another day."

"Right," she agreed, as she took a look at the nearby watches. Her eyebrows shot up. "These are pretty fancy."

"Some of them are, and some of them aren't," Danny explained. "Watches come in a wide range of selling prices. Just like women wear bracelets, men wear watches."

"Oh, that makes more sense. My husband had a huge collection of watches."

He asked her, "And you're thinking about giving Mack one of those for Christmas?"

"I would consider it, except that I'm really not sure they're the watches he would wear."

"And why is that?" he asked curiously.

She looked over at him and winced. "I think my husband paid hundreds of thousands of dollars for them."

He looked at her, blinked several times, and then nodded. "That's a very good point. I'm not sure that's necessarily what Mack is looking for. Yet that doesn't mean that he couldn't have two watches. Still, if you have that level of a watch at home, it's not the same watch that he might wear to work."

"That's the problem," she pointed out. "I really want him to have something that he'll use, not just put away, the way my late husband did."

"Did he really have many of them?"

"Multiples, so many of them," she said, "but I don't really know much more than that. We're doing a full accounting on them now."

"Right, he's since passed on, hasn't he?" Danny asked.

"Yes, he has, and I'm inheriting the estate, which means that the watches are coming my way too."

"Of course," he noted, with a nod. "If you ever decide you want to sell them, I would be happy to take a look at them."

"And I might have to," she said, with an eye roll. "I really don't even know what's there yet, so hold on to that thought a little bit longer."

"You know, Doreen, that is something to be seriously considered," he shared. "If he paid that much, some of those watches could even be collector's items."

She winced. "With my luck they will be." When he looked at her in astonishment, she sighed. "I know, it makes me sound very ungrateful, and I certainly am not," she said, holding up a hand. "It's just that, … once again, it's a field I don't know anything about. So I'm not sure what I should be doing or how I should handle it."

"That's why you hire professionals to handle it," he said, with a gentle smile. "You're doing everything right. You just need to give yourself time for the process to work."

"*Right*," she muttered.

"Now," he began, "let's focus on Mack and a watch that he can use for work. Do you know what color his is?"

"Silver," she said.

He nodded. "That's the bulk of them. Do you know what color the watch strap is?"

"Silver, … but I don't know but I think it's silver. I don't honestly know if it started that way or if it's just from wear. It's irritating his wrist now too, so whatever coating was on there is long gone."

"Does he ever mention what he likes in a watch?"

She shook her head. "That's one of the reasons why I don't even know if I should be looking at a watch. I mean, honestly, it all just feels very awkward."

"And that's okay too," Danny noted. "In our case, your purchase would be something he could bring back in and exchange, if he didn't like it."

"Oh," she said in delight. "That would make sense."

"Then you're not locked into making the wrong decision."

"No, I'm still locked into making the wrong decision," she clarified, "but he's not locked into having to like my wrong decision."

Danny burst out laughing at that logic. "Okay, I can live with that too."

It took a bit, but she did find a watch that she thought Mack would really like. By the time she had it on her credit card and clutched her purchase in her hand, she felt mighty proud of herself.

As she went to leave, Danny added, "And, if you do want somebody to go over those watches from your ex, you let me know."

"I'll think about it. That's a whole ball of wax that I don't even think I'm ready to open yet."

He nodded. "Some of these things take time, particularly when a death is involved. Don't rush yourself. Pack everything into a safe or put it away for a bit, and then you can always decide later."

She thanked him for his consideration, and, with the animals in tow, she moved toward the door. Then she stopped and asked, "Did you know Brandon Phelps?"

He frowned at her. "I don't think so. Why?"

"He was the guy who was killed in a semi-truck accident last week," she shared.

He shook his head. "It's not a name I know, but my condolences to the family. It's a tough time of year to lose somebody."

"Right, it just seems even more heartbreaking when it's Christmastime."

He nodded.

"He knew somebody named Pengo or Potter or something odd." She frowned.

"Oh, him." Danny winced. "Yeah, he's not somebody I even want in my store. I don't have any proof, but I'm pretty sure he stole from me way back when. It was one of the reasons I upgraded the security systems."

"Ah, that makes more sense. Brandon apparently did time based on something that the other guy did instead."

"I wouldn't be at all surprised if Pengo did that. I don't think he's necessarily dangerous though," he added quickly. "He was just slimy, you know? A shyster."

"That isn't good either," she muttered.

"No, it sure isn't, and it causes all kinds of destruction in the business world," he added, with a smile.

"It is frustrating," she muttered. "I mean, people can do so many good things with their lives, and yet what do they end up doing? They end up robbing people who are just trying to make an honest living. Have you seen this Pengo guy lately?"

"No, I don't think so, not in a very long time." Danny eyed her curiously. "Is this another case?"

"Everybody keeps asking me that," she said, with a

smile. "It's not really a case. I was just thinking how sad it was that Brandon died before he could get the Freedom Project to take his case and to help clear his name."

"If it was something that he didn't do, you would think that they would do it, even *in absentia.*"

"I did talk to them, but they have very limited man-hours and money, so must choose the cases they take on very carefully. They were certainly sympathetic," she noted, "but it wasn't something that they could see themselves picking up and moving forward with. She pointed out that they had thousands of cases waiting to be dealt with. That is quite a hefty wait list."

"Ouch." Danny shivered. "I don't know anything specifically about the man in question. I just know that Pengo's not somebody I want back around here again." Then he held up one finger. "I think his sister, Miriam, works at that fancy restaurant next to the food court shops in the mall."

"Oh, that's interesting," Doreen noted, turning to look at him.

"Oh, no. You'll go off and talk to her, won't you?" he asked, with a laugh.

"I probably will. I guess nobody else cares, but it does bother me that this Brandon is dead and gone and served time for a B&E he didn't do, and nobody will ever know the difference."

"Not to mention the fact that the other guy got away with the crime."

"Exactly." She nodded, appreciating the fact that Danny at least understood. "I've never really been a fan of people getting away with things, especially with blaming other people for something they did and somehow managing to walk."

"Right? That's always the worst," he muttered. "I think she might even own her restaurant." He stopped for a moment and thought about it, then added, "I don't remember what it's called, but it's a nice restaurant, next to all the food court shops, as you walk in."

"Oh, I think I've been in there."

"It's expensive, so …"

"In that case, I haven't been there," Doreen corrected, with an eye roll. "I haven't exactly been shopping much."

"At least now you can look forward to buying what you need, when your ex's estate is settled," he pointed out.

"Maybe so. Anyway, thanks for your help." And, with a smile, she waved and headed back to her car with the animals. They'd been incredibly well behaved while she'd been in the store, but she wasn't sure she could count on their cooperation much longer. So she headed over to a small park close by and let everybody get out and wander a little bit. If nothing else, this break would keep them pacified, as she ran her errands.

As they were wandering, she saw several other people walking around too. It was just that kind of a day, cold but refreshing.

Another woman smiled at her and laughed when she saw the animals. "I haven't ever seen you here before," she said, as she walked over with her dog.

Mugs and the dog sniffed each other several times and then, almost by mutual agreement, seemed to walk away from each other, as if that was it. They'd had their conversation and had now moved on.

Doreen laughed. "I don't quite understand how they sort out who they should talk to longer and who to ignore, but it sure seems as if they do it mutually."

"I know," the other woman confessed. "I've tried to figure it out but finally just gave up."

Doreen nodded. "Giving up figuring out our animals would make more sense, yet my curiosity is always there, telling me that I'm missing something and that, if I would just pay more attention, I would understand them better."

"If you say so," she replied, laughing. "The more I try to figure it out, the more confused I get."

Doreen continued to watch as the animals wandered around, seemingly having a happy little visit with each other and with whatever trees and bushes seemed to attract their attention.

The other woman looked over at Doreen and asked, "Do I know you?"

"I don't think so," Doreen replied absentmindedly, still focused on that expensive restaurant in the mall that Danny had mentioned. Doreen smiled at the lady with the dog. "I'm Doreen."

The woman's face lit up. "Oh, in that case, I do know you."

"Oh? In a good way or a bad way?"

The other woman went off in peals of laughter. "In a good way. I've certainly heard about the animals." Then she turned and looked at them. "Are these the ones forever getting in trouble?" she asked in fascination.

Doreen winced. "Yes, here they are," she replied glumly. "Lots of people don't particularly like to see me coming because the animals get into trouble."

"Oh, but you come from the heart, and you help a lot of people by solving these cases," she noted, with a smile, and then she looked around. "Are you on a case right now?" She had lowered her voice, as if afraid somebody would hear her.

Doreen winced. "No, I'm just out walking the animals."

"Right." Still, the woman had a knowing grin on her face.

Doreen figured the woman would likely go home and chat with her friends about seeing Doreen and her animals. "Honestly, I'm just here getting a little fresh air."

"Good." The woman smiled. "That's important too."

Chapter 13

DOREEN PONDERED THE weird visit as she continued walking her animals in the park. It seemed as if some people were very comfortable around her and her pets, while others were just the opposite. She wasn't sure what she did or could do to put people at ease, but it seemed sometimes she did. Yet other times she somehow hit a nerve, and people just took off, unsure what to say to her.

She got back in her vehicle, and Mugs started to *woof* beside her. She looked over at him. "What's the matter, bud?" Not sure anything was the matter, she figured he wanted food. "Oh, food, yeah. You smelled some nearby restaurant, didn't you?" Just then her stomach rumbled. She groaned. "We could head to the food court in the mall and see if there is anything of interest," she muttered. Plus, she wanted to find Pengo's sister's business as well.

He barked again.

"Right, the trouble is, you're always happy to get me into trouble, but Mack won't be very happy if I do interfere in his current investigation," she muttered.

Mugs barked again, as if in complete agreement. However, as far as she was concerned, it was an agreement that she was doing okay, not that she shouldn't go into the mall.

Smiling, she drove toward the mall but then realized she couldn't take all her animals inside a food establishment, unless the store had an outside eating area. Sure enough, as she pulled up to the side, she saw that it did, indeed.

She hopped out, looked at Mugs, and asked, "So, you want to go there?"

He pulled on his leash, eager to head inside. Goliath just stared at her. "Your leash is required. Otherwise you'll have to stay in the car."

He wailed at that, and she would be the first one to say she was maybe starting to lose it. If that was what it looked like, maybe she had. With a bright smile she put Goliath on his leash and perched Thaddeus on her shoulder, as she headed to the front door.

As she opened it and stepped inside, a woman turned toward her and her animals, and an expression of complete distaste crossed her face. Doreen nodded. "I guess that means we're not welcome in here, are we?"

The woman replied, "Can you guarantee that they won't leave a mess?"

"They haven't left a mess yet," Doreen stated, "but I can certainly understand if this makes you uncomfortable. I was looking for a place outside to sit, but it's cold."

"I'm not much of an animal lover," she admitted, as she stared at them, trying to hide the disgust in her tone but failing completely.

"Right," Doreen noted. "In that case we can leave. I just came hoping to see a woman called Miriam."

The woman frowned at her. "I'm Miriam."

"Oh, I just wondered where your brother was. I was trying to get a hold of him."

At that, a cautious look came across her face. "Why?"

"I was told he was the person I needed to talk to," Doreen replied. "Is that a problem?" She really tried to infuse enough guile into her tone that nobody would understand what she was up to. It was getting to be a bit of a handicap having the animals with her all the time, or at least being recognized with the animals, because that gave her away as the detective lady.

Miriam hesitated, then shared, "I think he's at work."

"Oh, and where does he work?" she asked.

She shrugged. "At the equipment rental place."

"Okay, any idea when he gets off? I really do want to talk to him."

Miriam frowned. "I'm not sure what your business dealing is with him, but he's pretty busy."

"I'm sure he is. Still, that won't change the fact that I need to talk to him." Miriam glared at her, and Doreen just smiled. "Unless, of course, there's a problem."

"No, of course not," Miriam snapped in exasperation. "It's not as if you're telling me anything."

"It's not as if I need to though, do I?" Doreen asked, eyeing her in astonishment. "It's your brother I need to talk to."

Miriam finally conceded, "Okay, you can probably text him."

"That would be good, but I don't have his number. If you could share that with me, that would be awesome." Miriam seemed frozen, and Doreen just studied her curiously. "I'm not coming after him for anything, and I'm way too old to be chasing anybody like that."

She laughed. "Are you kidding? He would take anybody at this stage. He's been single for a while. Never really a state

I understood."

Doreen just nodded, not sure whether the woman would give up Pengo's number or not.

Finally Miriam sighed. "Whatever. I'm not his keeper." And, with that, she handed over his phone number. "If he gets mad at me, I'll just blame it on your animals."

"Sure," Doreen agreed, with a smile, and then thanked her, exiting quickly. Sometimes the animals helped, but, in many cases, they made life even more difficult for her. Yet today seemed to be a good day. She headed back to her vehicle, only to have Mugs give a long petulant howl, and she realized that he thought visiting the food court would be part of the outing.

"Sorry, buddy. I think we need to head home." He gave another howl, and she groaned. "I won't give in to that," she muttered. "No way I can." He gave her his woeful expression, and she sighed. "We can hit a drive-through, but that's it."

His tail started to wag, and she realized what a monster she'd created. A few months ago she'd stopped at the drive-through of one of the coffee shops. She was asked if she wanted to get her dog a pup cup, something she'd never even heard of. Sadly now Mugs seemed to think that every time they were in the car that a treat was in it for him.

"I shouldn't let you get away with this," she muttered, but he'd saved her so many times and had been such a blessing, it was really hard for her to be a hardnose about it.

Groaning, she headed to the closest drive-through, and, as soon as she got there, she ordered him a pup cup. Immediately her stomach growled again, and she was getting ravenously hungry. So she picked up a sandwich for herself. As she drove home, she muttered, "That was just silly. I could have made a sandwich at home."

He woofed as he sniffed the pup cup, trying eagerly to get to it. "Oh, no you don't," she muttered. "We're going home to have it."

Which really didn't make any sense because the whole point of a pup cup was to have it while they were out. She groaned, and, by the time she was parked, he was misbehaving to the point that she didn't want to give him anything. Yet he calmed down when they got into the house and then sat beautifully, while she held it out to him. He scarfed it up in seconds. Afterward, he danced around in joy, making her laugh, then curled up on his day bed and fell asleep. She stared at him, smiling at his antics.

Her phone rang a few minutes later, and, as soon as she answered, a man asked, "What did you want with me?"

She stared down at the phone and asked, "Who is this?"

"You're the one who sent me a text."

"Oh, right. I'm just now at home."

"Whatever. What do you want?"

"I wondered if you knew about your friend who has passed away, Brandon Phelps."

The rude man went silent for a moment. "He's dead?" he asked.

Something was off in his tone. "Yes," Doreen confirmed. "He's dead. I'm so sorry."

"How did you know that we were friends?" he asked.

"I inherited a box of materials from him, and your name was mentioned a few times," she shared. "I haven't really had a chance to go through very much of it yet, but I figured you probably hadn't heard. So I wanted to confirm that you knew."

"You're right. I hadn't heard."

"I'm sorry. It's always tough to hear news like that."

"Yeah, you're not kidding," he muttered. "So you say you inherited a box …"

"Yeah, just some of his keepsakes and things and papers from some court case. I think he was working on trying to clear his name. I haven't really had a chance to sort through it all, but I did see your name mentioned on the paperwork as somebody he knew well. So, I just thought maybe I would give you a shout and let you know about his demise." Then she just waited.

"Thank you for that. … Nobody ever tells people these things. Since I don't do social media, it's not as if posting it would help me out."

"Right. I'm not big on social media either."

With that, he rang off without another word.

"Darn it, Mack'll be pissed off that I got to Pengo first about this," she muttered to herself. Of course it had been sheer instincts to have an honest talk with him, but that would mean something completely different to Mack. She sent him a text and waited.

When Mack phoned a few minutes later, he asked, "What are you up to?"

Such wariness filled his tone that she sighed. "It would be so much nicer if every time you asked that question it didn't sound as if you were expecting the world to collapse."

He snorted. "It would also be awesome if I could ask that question and not be holding my breath, wondering if the world was about to collapse."

"I guess I'm just a trial, aren't I?" she asked in a sad tone.

"Ha. You won't catch me with that question. Nope, not touching it. So, what have you been up to?"

"How do you know I've been up to anything?"

"For one thing, you're stalling, which means you're up to something, and, two, it's you."

She groaned. "Yet it's Christmastime, and, as everybody keeps telling me, you're not supposed to ask a ton of questions because you might find out more than you should. Plus, I haven't been up to anything." She hoped her sunny tone would throw him off, not make him more suspicious.

"I should get off work at a decent hour tonight," he shared. "How do you feel about dinner? If I get tied up, we can always do dinner tomorrow night."

"Dinner tonight or tomorrow night sounds wonderful," she replied. "I just picked up a sandwich, so I can wait for dinner, even if you are late."

"Where did you go?" he asked.

She sighed. "Remember that thing about not asking questions?"

"You won't get away with saying that for much longer," he noted, a sharpness in his tone. "Christmas is right around the corner, and, after that, you don't get to use that excuse anymore."

"Oh." She would have to think about that. "I guess that makes sense."

"Yes, it makes sense," he agreed, a note of laughter in his tone.

"In the meantime, I'll keep using it while I can." And, with that, she ended the call.

Chapter 14

THE NEXT MORNING, Doreen had just gotten up and had her shower and got dressed, when Mack called her. "Enjoyed dinner last night."

"Me too. You are such a good cook."

Mack laughed. "Are you ready for the party?"

"Oh, gosh, I don't know that I'm ready for all that attention. And I still don't have any live mistletoe for the party. Nan will be disappointed. I don't think Nan feels as if she's ready either, and she's really put her heart and soul into this thing. I just wish I knew why she cared so much about this whole charade."

"I would guess, at the heart of it is, … she cares about you an awful lot."

"I know. I know," she muttered. "I'm just anxious about being the center of attention at this party. But because she cares, I'll be there, doing everything I can to make it easier on her. But she won't explain why she's so stressed out, and that bothers me."

"Really?" He laughed. "With everything else going on in this world, *that's* what bothers you?"

"I just get the feeling that she's up to something."

"And remember what you told me last night?"

"What?" she asked.

"It's Christmas, and you're not allowed to ask questions. Secrets and all. I've been waiting for a chance to say that back at you," he said, still chuckling.

"I don't know," she muttered, frowning at her phone. "This doesn't feel like the same thing."

"Let it go, and, if she wants to tell you what she's up in arms about, she will."

"That's exactly what she would tell me. You are getting to know Nan very well."

"Yep. I try."

"I was hoping we could get this party over and done with, and then maybe she wouldn't feel quite so stressed."

"I'm sure that's true for her as well," he noted.

Still, she caught an odd note in his tone. "You guys better not be conniving something together."

He started to laugh. "*Conniving?*"

"Whatever that word is when people get together and create things that upset other people."

He sighed. "I have no idea what's in your mind. Nan's actions could mean all kinds of things. What about my brother? Did he get a hold of you?"

She blinked at the sudden turn of conversation. "I've talked to him multiple times. Every time I hear his voice, I cringe."

"Why?" Mack asked. "He's solving all kinds of problems for you, isn't he?"

"Sure. And then we have more stuff to do to tie up Mathew's estate."

By the time he ended the call, her mind was already working on what she would do next with Brandon's cold case. She also needed to go help Nan this afternoon with whatever was left on her to-do list.

The party was only one day away, and she was still nervous about it, uncertain how she was supposed to act at these things. At least she had a Christmas gift for Mack, but they would exchange gifts privately. Wouldn't they? She would ask him the next time they talked. At least his gift was taken care of.

When Nick called soon afterward, this time it was a happy message, as he had found out that her great-great-grandmother's necklace was among Mathew's estate. So Doreen asked to have that sent to her, so that she would have that as a Christmas surprise for Nan.

Did she need to buy gifts for other people? With Richie, Doreen could get some of those special chocolates he really liked but never seemed to get enough of. She immediately headed out to pick up that and various items for other people, like Wendy. By the time Doreen was done, she had made quite a few purchases. However, back at home again, she groaned. She didn't have paper to wrap anything with.

Nan called around that time, and Doreen smiled. "Hey, Nan. I think I've managed to buy Christmas gifts, but I don't have any wrapping paper. I didn't even think of that when I was out shopping."

"You can certainly come down here and use mine," Nan offered.

"I probably have too many for that to make sense. I'll go back out and grab some."

"You can always stop by here afterward," Nan added. "It would be nice to see you."

A wistfulness filled her tone that Doreen wasn't used to hearing. "I planned to come help with whatever is still on your party to-do list. I'll pick up wrapping paper on the way. I wonder if Wendy has any."

Nan asked, "Wendy? Consignment store, Wendy?"

"Yeah, she sells all kinds of interesting things there."

"I see." Then Nan added in a very gentle tone, "You do know you have money now, right?"

"Meaning?"

"I just don't want you to be deliberately not spending money or pinching pennies because you still have that *I don't have money* mentality."

"Nan, it's not as if I really have money yet," she clarified. "I know that some money is coming, and I know I've got a bunch more coming my way, but I haven't figured out what I'm supposed to do with it yet," she shared carefully. "So I don't want to spend it foolishly, not until I know I have a nest egg set aside for the rest of my life and yours."

"Right," Nan muttered.

Doreen noted an odd tone in Nan's voice. "You sound as if I've disappointed you."

"Never, child, never," she replied warmly. "If anything, you are very true to form. Anyway, go get your wrapping paper, and, if you want, you can come help me wrap my gifts, then do some party stuff afterward. I'll be right here."

"Sure, I can do that, but, … if you want your gifts to look very good, you might need to do it yourself."

Nan burst into peals of laughter. "It's just gifts for friends and family."

"I know, but, Nan, I don't think I've ever wrapped a gift before."

"Oh, good Lord," she said in astonishment. "Get your wrapping paper and get yourself down here. We'll have to fix that right away."

Wincing at that, Doreen quickly loaded up the animals, took them down to the corner store, which was more of a housewares store, not quite a dollar store but similar—maybe a couple-of-dollars store, if there was such a thing. By the time she had wrapping paper in hand, pretty Christmassy stuff, she was starting to feel a whole lot better.

She headed down to Nan's, and she walked inside her grandmother's apartment, Nan giving her and her animals some hugs. Then she took one look at the paper and smiled in delight.

"Oh, good choice. I was afraid you would come back with happy birthday paper."

Doreen frowned at her grandmother. "Am I that bad?"

Nan winced, "Sometimes, … yes."

"Oh, good Lord," Doreen muttered. "In that case I won't give you any of these." With that threat, she dangled her second attempt at shortbreads in front of her grandmother.

Nan looked at them and nodded. "How many times have you tried to make them so far?"

"Twice."

"*Hmm.*"

"Why? Are you thinking they're not worth sharing yet?" she asked warily.

"In your case you might need a third or fourth time." Doreen glared at her, but Nan cheerfully swiped the bag from her hand and laughed. "No need to be fussy. We'll get Richie to try them. He eats anything."

"They can't be that bad," she wailed. "I was thinking I would give Mack some cookies for Christmas."

"Sure, but you should buy them."

At that, Doreen stopped to glare at Nan, only to find her

chortling with laughter at having delivered such a comeuppance. "You'll make me feel as if I can't cook anything."

"I won't say you can, and I certainly won't say you can't because, of course, … it is a learned thing. So, as long as you keep practicing, you'll probably end up doing just fine."

"It's the *probably* that gets me every time you open your mouth."

"It ends up getting me a little bit sometimes too," Nan admitted, with a smile. "Anyway, let's not fight over your cookies. I'm sure they're fine."

Doreen looked at the bag dolefully, but then they started wrapping gifts. It didn't take her long to get the hang of it. Thankfully her animals were all napping and on their best behavior. She worked through the bulk of her own gifts that she had brought, after leaving the ones for Nan and Mack at home. She was just about done when Richie popped his head through the open door.

He frowned at her. "Oh, I thought I smelled cookies."

Nan laughed. "You did, indeed. I also texted you that there were cookies."

He rolled his eyes. "I was trying to be discreet. So where are they?" he asked, looking around. "Your grandmother doesn't think you can make anything decent, so I'm here to taste them.'

"*Great,*" Doreen muttered under her breath, glaring at their grinning faces. "You two don't do very much for my self-confidence."

"No," he agreed, "but then you're not doing a whole lot for ours either." With a delightful expression on his face, he took a big bite. He tilted his head to one side and then the other, finally nodding. "They're not bad, Doreen."

"But they're not good," she muttered, her shoulders falling in defeat.

"It's not that," he countered, "not at all. I would say, … you need a light hand with shortbread. You know that, right? They can get really tough if you don't."

"How does a cookie get tough?" she asked, staring at the déjà vu moment, since Mack had given her the same review.

"You overkneaded it. Shortbreads are delicate."

"Delicate," she repeated. She stared at him, then at her grandmother. "You really did bring him over to check and see if they were edible, didn't you?"

Nan picked up one, took a bite, considered it, and agreed, "You just need to learn to handle it lighter."

"Lighter? I barely touched them."

"Did you use my recipe?" Nan asked.

"No, I didn't use your recipe. I used one off the internet."

"Then I would say that's also part of the problem," Nan noted. "I have the most melt-in-your-mouth recipe ever."

"*Sure*," Doreen uttered, followed by a heavy sigh.

"I mean it," Nan declared.

"Fine," Doreen conceded. "I'll look for it when I get home."

Nan shook her head, whipped out her phone, and quickly emailed her the recipe. "Try using that, definitely *before* you give them to Mack."

"They're that bad?" she asked, her shoulders sagging again.

"No, not at all," Richie said. "We just want to see more samples before you feed it to your man." And, with a grin, Richie snagged up yet another one and scarfed it down.

By now Doreen wasn't sure if any of these reviews were for real or not. "*Fine*," she muttered, as she looked at them.

"I'll try again."

"Good. I'm always here for you," Richie vowed, a hand over his heart. "Honestly, we'll make sure that you get these cookies right by the time you're done."

"*Right*." She glared at him. "It'll probably take me six batches."

"Oh, it could," he agreed, nodding vigorously. "It absolutely could. You should probably go home and get started."

She sighed, not sure if he was joking again or whether she was the butt of a serious joke. Still, she knew something was definitely amiss, and she should go home and work on her baking skills. "Fine. I did buy enough ingredients to try another batch."

"Good," Nan said, patting her on the shoulder. "Time for you to leave then."

Doreen eyed her, surprised. "I thought you wanted help with the party preparations."

"Oh, no, child. They're all done now. The party is the day after tomorrow." Then she faced her, frowning, and added, "Do you have something special to wear?"

Her jaw dropped. "You mean I have to dress up too?"

"Of course you do." Nan's tone suggested how naive she thought her granddaughter was. "It's a Christmas party, child."

"Right," Doreen said dolefully. "In that case, I'm not sure."

"Find something nice to wear. That's your job for the next twenty-four hours," Nan ordered.

"And bake cookies," Richie reminded her in a hopeful tone.

"*Fine*, play dress-up and bake cookies. Just what I need. On that note," she said, standing now, "I'll take my leave and go home."

"Good idea," Richie agreed, chortling.

She looked at him and glared. "You're having way-too-much fun over this."

"I am, indeed," he confirmed, with a smile. "Sometimes that's just what it's all about, enjoying life and having fun."

"If you say so," Doreen muttered. "It feels as if it's not always a whole lot of fun on my side."

"But it will be," Richie stated, with a wave of his hand. "It absolutely will. You just have yet to get there." And, on that note, he took off for his apartment.

Doreen looked over at Nan. "Really? You're sure the cookies are that bad?"

"They're not that bad, child, but, in a world where shortbread should melt in your mouth and should be absolutely delicious," she explained, "this batch would probably be about a six or seven out of ten."

"Oh, … okay, got it."

"Don't be hurt. It's for your own good. Anyone who can make a serious batch of shortbread can have any man she wants."

"Goodness." She turned to face her grandmother. "Why on earth would I care?"

Her grandmother shook her head. "Child, you are a challenge sometimes."

"I know you want to get me married off," Doreen noted, "but I'm really, really enjoying being single."

"I know that," Nan replied, "but you're also coming at it from a much younger space than I am."

"Maybe, and maybe that's a good space to be coming from," she pointed out. "It's not as if you were married for long and chose to never remarry, even though I know you were proposed to more than once."

"No, I never remarried," she confirmed, "but neither was I alone all the time either."

Not a whole lot Doreen could say about that. Besides, when it came to arguments with Nan, Doreen always lost anyway. She turned around to see where Goliath was, only to find him on the table, knocking cookies onto the floor, where Mugs scarfed them up, two at a time. "Wait, wait, wait," she cried out.

Goliath sat down, reached for the last cookie with his paw, waited until she almost got there, and knocked it onto the floor. Mugs didn't wait long for anything and had it in his mouth, and it was gone instantly.

She turned and glared at Nan, who was laughing uproariously, holding her sides. "I'm glad you think it's so funny."

"Of course it is. It's absolutely awesome," Nan crowed. "Think of it. Mugs seems to love your baking."

Her defeat must have shown because her grandmother came over and hugged her. "We're doing this for your benefit, child."

"Sure, you are," Doreen said, topped off with an eye roll. "Somehow it doesn't feel as if this is for my benefit. This feels very much like it's for your entertainment."

"Of course not." Nan chuckled. "We love you."

"Right." And on that note she headed out to her car, with her animals, Mugs waddling now, a little heavier than when he arrived. She glared down at him. "That is not what was supposed to happen to those cookies," she muttered. He looked up at her with the most innocent of looks and woofed several times. "Right, as if you care."

He woofed again, and she groaned because he didn't care. It was a cookie after all. And, for that matter, Mack probably wouldn't have cared either. But now she felt as if she had to go home and do better. Yet, how does one do better? That didn't make a whole lot of sense to her. As far as she was concerned, she really had tried.

"Lighter," she repeated. "It has to be lighter." But what she probably really needed to do was check Nan's recipe. At least if she used that one, and she showed them how it could or could not turn out, then maybe it would pass their inspection quite nicely. She wasn't even sure what that meant, but she was all about giving it one more try.

"But only one more time," she stated. Mugs looked at her and woofed. "No, not for you," she declared. "You've had your shot. You've had enough for everyone."

He woofed several more times, and she shook her head, "I know more of your tricks now. Not happening, buddy."

Chapter 15

Back home, Doreen unloaded the car and the rest of the wrapping paper that hadn't been used, stowed away her wrapped gifts in a closet with the door securely shut, so that nobody could get into it, and brought out her recipe from Nan. It didn't look to be any harder or any more difficult, but there was a word of warning about a gentle hand making all the difference. "*Fine*," she muttered.

She quickly whipped up a batch, making sure that she was extremely gentle with it. It was darn hard to mix anything if you had to be gentle though. She was beyond frustrated by the time she got it into the oven, basically holding her breath the whole time to confirm it would not fall or do something silly. She knew shortbread cookies weren't supposed to fall, but, in her case, where life happened for reasons completely unknown to her, things fell.

She stood by the stove, watching intently as they cooked. By the time she had read the instructions on how long to cook them and how long to keep them on a cooling rack, she realized that it was already time to pull out the first pan. She took them out ever-so-carefully, and she put in a second cookie sheet. By the time those were done and the third and final batch were in, she felt a little calmer.

As she took them off the cooling racks, she turned to see a stranger standing in her kitchen. She frowned at him. "Good Lord," she said in shock. "How did you get in?"

She looked down at Mugs, but his attention was on the cookies. He turned, looked at the newcomer, woofed several times, then focused again on the cookies. "Seriously, Mugs, what kind of a watchdog are you?"

The stranger snorted. "Seriously? That's a watchdog? Looks like one big cookie-eating monster to me."

"I know." She glared down at the dog. "How did you get in?" she asked the stranger again.

"What do you mean, how did I get in?" He frowned at her. "I opened the door."

"Did you ring the doorbell?"

"Did you hear a doorbell?"

"No, I didn't hear a doorbell," she snapped, glaring at him.

"Then I guess I didn't ring a doorbell, did I? Good Lord," he muttered. "What kind of question is that?"

She laughed at him. "Good Lord, what a …"

He froze and glared at her.

She could see all sense of good humor falling away. "You're the one who came into my house without permission," she explained. "So you don't get to be upset because I'm laughing at you."

"*Sure*," he snapped, his tone harsh, as he stared at her. "And you're the one who has files that I'm looking for."

She nodded. "Oh, so you're Pengo."

He continued to glare at her.

Doreen added, "If you'd just asked, we could have started this conversation more amicably."

"I would have, if you'd answered the door."

She frowned at that. "And I would have, if you would have knocked."

He just rolled his eyes. "I really need to see what he had in the files."

"Why?" she asked, her gaze on the clock.

Finally he got irritated at her and asked, "What are you doing staring at the clock all the time? If you're looking for some rescue, it's not happening."

She turned and faced him, one eyebrow up. "Why do I need a rescue? And, for your information, I'm watching the cookies' timer."

"What cookies?" And then he sniffed the air and smiled. "Shortbread."

"Yeah, apparently they're an iconic Christmas thing."

"Of course they are," he declared. "Everybody has shortbreads at Christmas."

"How can that be if I didn't get shortbreads at Christmas?"

"Oh, sorry," he quipped in a mocking tone. "My heart bleeds, and I feel so bad for you."

"Yeah, *bad* is right," she said. "This is now the third time making them, and I want them to turn out perfect."

"It depends if you overkneaded them."

"I did *not* overknead them," she snapped, glaring at this person who'd just walked into her house and already appeared to know more about shortbreads than she did. "Is everybody a bloody expert on shortbreads?"

"Yeah, pretty well," he stated, with a nod. "You would have to be if you want to make them right."

"It doesn't matter," she snapped, glaring at him. "And I don't have any files."

"You told me you had files from Brandon Phelps."

"I have the box of stuff that I got from him, sure," she clarified, "but, as it turns out, it's a dud. It ended up being mostly garbage and then some information on that court case. Not much, just that he was trying to clear his name."

"Interesting," he muttered. "So where is it?"

"Why?" she asked, turning to look at him. "It's not yours. It's mine."

He raised his eyebrows. "Except that you said my name was in there."

"Yes, so what? That's how I found you, so I could let you know that Brandon was gone. Now that he's gone, it shouldn't matter what name is in the file."

"Maybe. But you never know when some crazy do-gooders around this place might decide something needs to be done to clear his name, even though he's dead and gone. You know that this crazy animal lady is in town here, and she gets into all kinds of trouble with old cases and all."

Doreen flushed, wondering if he would make the connection or not.

When he stopped and added, "She's got all these animals, something about a dog—so I would almost think it was you—except there's no bird."

At that exact moment, Thaddeus poked his head out from under her long hair. "Thaddeus is here. Thaddeus is here." As Pengo fell back in surprise, Thaddeus lifted his wings and squawked at him several times.

"Good God," he muttered, "it is you."

"I don't think Thaddeus takes kindly to you, talking about me like that," she replied in her primmest tone.

"Really? As if I care." She glared at him, and he nodded. "I mean it, as if I care. Now, where's that file?" She slammed her foot down, and he laughed. "Better not do that. The shortbreads will fall." Immediately she opened the oven to check her baking cookies, and he burst out laughing. "Good God, you really don't know the first things about cooking."

"That's not fair," she protested. "I've been learning."

"Seems you've got a long way to go." He shook his head. "I pity any guy who hooks up with you. You couldn't even put a decent meal on the table."

And that, for some reason, stung. "I'm getting much better," she declared, glaring at him. "And it's none of your business if I can put a meal on the table or not."

"No, it really isn't because I really don't care. Now where is that file?"

She walked past him, pulled out the envelope she had at the ready, and handed it to him. "There. That's all that's relevant. I chucked the rest of the box of stuff because it was nothing related. He had duplicates, but I don't know what his intentions were. I guess he would mail it off to somebody or something."

"Yeah, he would do something stupid like that," Pengo noted in disgust.

She turned and immediately checked on the shortbread again.

"You can't keep opening the oven door like that," he shared in disgust. "You're letting all the heat out."

She closed the oven door, then turned back to him. "I can't tell if you're having fun at my expense or if you're serious."

He frowned at her, and then shook his head. "I can't even believe I'm having this conversation with you."

"Neither can I," she snapped. "Now that you've got what you wanted, why don't you just take a hike?"

"Yeah, I'm happy to," he said, shaking his head. "Have fun with your shortbreads—or not." And, with that, he was gone.

She groaned and looked down at Mugs. "I'm not sure you should have any more treats. You didn't care even that he was in here or not." Mugs just stared at her. She almost heard him thinking, *Yeah, but he was harmless, so who cares?* Then he jumped up on his back legs and sniffed the counter where the cookies were cooling. "Oh no you don't," she declared. "That is not happening."

Mack walked in just then, sniffed the room, and asked, "Good God, what are you making?"

Her shoulders sank. "You didn't say that in the tone of *Oh my goodness, that smells absolutely wonderful.*" She shook her head at him. "So that means it smells terrible."

"No," he said gently, as he walked over, wrapped her up in a hug, and added, "It means that I don't recognize the smell."

"Seriously? I thought these are supposed to be iconic."

His gaze landed on the cookies on the counter, and his face lit up. "Shortbread. Again."

"How come everybody knows what shortbread looks like?"

"Because we all grew up with them." Still holding her, he walked her backward several steps, so he'd get close enough to snag one. When he popped it into his mouth, he closed his eyes, and a look of sheer delight filled his face.

She fidgeted nervously, watching him for a long moment. When he didn't say anything, her shoulders sagged.

He looked down at her, a quizzical expression on his face. "What kind of reaction is that?"

"Maybe that's a better question for you," she muttered.

"I was hoping for some a sign that it was decent."

"Good Lord, of course they're decent. They're better than decent." He took another bite and then another. "Oh my," he muttered, "these are so addictive." He reached behind her again and snagged two more.

She watched them each go down the hatch in what appeared to be a single swallow each. He looked back at the cookies, then at her. She shook her head. "Oh no you don't. That's my third batch. I've been trying so hard to make a decent shortbread, and now I don't even know whether I did it or not."

He stopped, stunned. "Who told you that you didn't make a decent shortbread?"

"Nan and Richie."

An odd look crossed his face. "Oh," he said, with a smirk.

"Why? What does that mean?"

He chuckled and then his chuckles went into huge guffaws. "Because I was just down there, and the two of them were apparently selling … care to guess what?"

"*Shortbread.*" Doreen gasped. "They wouldn't?"

"Yep, they would. I told them that the cookies looked really good, but Nan said that I wasn't allowed any. In fact, she told me that I would have to come to you and to get some myself." He started to laugh at the look on her face.

She stared at him. "Are you serious? Are you telling me that my own grandmother did that to me?"

He couldn't stop laughing, and he was now howling.

She snatched up her phone and called her grandmother. When Nan answered, Doreen asked, "Did you tell me that my cookies weren't good and that I had to come home and make more so that you could sell them off?"

Silence came from the other end. Then Nan started to chuckle. "I was bloody serious, child. You could have made better ones."

"I might have made better ones, but, if you think you're getting any after you've pulled that stunt," Doreen declared, "forget it." She ended the call without another word, still staring down at the phone in ire. She looked over at Mack, who'd already pilfered another couple cookies, so she glared at him now. "If you eat all those cookies, you're making the next batch."

He nodded agreeably. "I can do that."

"I spent all day making cookies, and Nan told me that they were too tough and that I worked the dough too much."

He stopped. "Oh."

"What do you mean, *Oh?*"

"It is a problem," he said. "No doubt about it. You can overdo the dough, and a light hand is definitely the best. Still, I highly suspect she was either making more out of it than you imagine or she just really wanted to tease you."

"Tease me?" Doreen repeated. "I thought they were horrible cookies. I wanted to make you cookies for Christmas, and she seemed to think that they were terrible."

Still trying to smother his laughter, he walked over, snagged her into his arms, twirled her around, and gave her a shortbread-tasting kiss. "Don't ever change." Just then Mugs gave a *woof,* and Mack bent down and gave him a piece of cookie.

"Oh no, he doesn't get any more cookies," she ordered. "He didn't do his job today."

Mack and Mugs shared a glance, then both turned to look at her. "What do you mean, he didn't do his job?"

Mack asked.

She winced. "Nothing. It was just a comment."

"Oh, no, no, no, no." Mack straightened up and glared at her. "What did you mean?"

"I didn't mean anything," she replied in exasperation. "I'm just upset at everybody having fun with my cookies."

"Fun with your cookies, which they're busy selling to raise money?"

"But what are they raising money for?"

"I have no clue," he admitted, with a headshake. "I just know I wasn't allowed to take part, and they wouldn't accept my money for whatever it is they were hoarding the money for."

"Oh, dear." Doreen sighed. "That woman will be the death of me."

He looked over at her and, with a chuckle, added, "I know the sentiment."

She glared. "I haven't done anything like that."

"No, but you're also trying very hard to avoid telling me what the heck is going on and why Mugs didn't do his job."

Mugs barked at that.

Doreen replied, patting Mugs now, "I know. I know. You thought he wasn't dangerous, so you didn't have to do anything. I get that, and maybe you're right. Maybe it's just me."

Mack stared at her. "Out with it now!" She remained silent, but Mack shook his head, planting his hands on his hips. "No, no, no. You're not getting out of explaining this one."

"It's nothing," she finally said.

"If it was nothing, you wouldn't be sitting there, arguing with Mugs."

"Yes, I would," she stated. "He's really easy to argue with."

"Heaven help me," he muttered.

"Yeah, you should be so lucky," she muttered, as she sat down at the table where the cookies were cooling, checked them over. She saw one that might be soft and fluffy and picked it up and took a bite.

"Now," Mack shared, "the test of shortbread is … will it melt in your mouth?"

And, in fact, all that buttery goodness was melting all over her taste buds, and she almost moaned in joy.

He nodded. "See? That's the sign of a good cookie." She stared at him around the mouthful, and it was gone in seconds. He chuckled. "You'll become a shortbread nut just like the rest of us."

She sighed. "How come I didn't know there was such a thing as shortbreads?"

"Mathew really didn't let you have any Christmas baking?"

"No. It would have made me fat, remember?"

His face darkened at that, and he pushed the whole platter of cookies in front of her, and said, "Eat to your heart's content."

She laughed. "The thing is, it's different when you can have it. I'm not necessarily even hungry. But these *are* really good." She finished the one in her hand and muttered, "I should have had it with coffee."

"That's okay. Now you can have coffee with a second one." She rolled her eyes at that. "But you're still not getting out of the issue at hand." She glared at him, and he nodded. "Oh, I know. I've gotten wind of most of your tricks by now. Every once in a while, you still avoid answering my questions on something. I don't get how I missed whatever it was that you were trying to hide from me, and you still do it a fair bit but not this time. So, what was Mugs supposed to do and yet didn't?"

"I won't get Mugs into trouble," she said. "That would be tattling."

He looked at her and grimaced. "You already tattled."

"Oh." She frowned and looked over at Mugs. "Sorry, buddy."

He woofed, as if to say, *That's okay. A cookie would fix it.*

She glared at him. "No, no more cookies."

"Doreen," Mack said in that urging tone of voice.

"Fine, fine, fine," she muttered, with a wave of her hand. "It's just that … somebody came by today. He didn't knock, or, if he did, I didn't hear it. I turned around, and he was in the kitchen already."

He frowned at her. "Who was it?"

"Pengo, the guy Brandon Phelps was trying to say was responsible for that B&E case he wanted the Freedom Project to get written off his records."

Mack sat down hard on the chair beside her. "He came here?"

"Yeah, not necessarily a good thing. Plus, I'm not exactly sure how he knew how to find me, outside of the fact that, according to Richard, it's hard *not* to find me."

"Good God." Mack stared at her. "Did you have a conversation with him?"

"Sure. What else could I do? He started off by telling me that my shortbreads were probably too tough." Mack's lips twitched at that. "Don't you start that again either."

"Did he try one?" he asked.

"No, I didn't let him try one. They were just coming out

of the oven, but, when I banged my foot on the floor, he told me the cookies would fall." At that, Mack started to laugh again. "And then I got really mad."

"Yeah, of course you would. And why did you get mad?"

"Because I didn't know whether he was telling the truth or not," she wailed in such a forlorn tone that Mack sighed, snagged her into his arms, and sat her on his lap.

"Did they look really high?" he asked.

"No." She turned to face him. "Does that mean they fell?"

"No," he replied, trying hard for calm and not an uproarious laughter. "It means that they wouldn't fall in the first place."

"Oh." She settled against his shoulder. "I guess people really do think I'm an idiot, don't they?"

"No, I think they find you incredibly endearing and lovely, and they aren't sure what they're supposed to do with you. Then, when they do find something, like the idea that you don't know about falling cookies," he clarified, his lips twitching once again, "I think it's instinctive for them to make fun of you."

"Maybe so," she muttered, "but it's not nice."

"No, it's not necessarily very nice," he said gently, "but you are learning every day."

"Sure, I might be learning, but that doesn't mean it's happening quick enough. I was thinking about taking cooking classes."

He shrugged. "If you would find that fun, then do it."

"I'm hoping that maybe it would be more than just fun, but it would also be useful."

"It would be useful," he said. "As long as you enjoy it, it would be useful. But you really don't need to do something you don't enjoy."

"Maybe, maybe not," she replied, throwing back her head, "because even if I don't enjoy it, that doesn't mean that I don't need to learn more basics. It is quite troubling that I can't do some of the most basic things."

"You just made shortbreads," he pointed out. "You made *fabulous* shortbreads, so it's not that you can't do some of the basic things. It's just like the shortbreads though, it might take you a time or two to learn it properly. And I've got to tell you how fabulous these are."

"But I wonder"—she turned to him, frowning—"if you would say that if they weren't mine."

"Meaning that I only like them because you made them?" he asked. "I must admit that they're extra special because I know you made them. Plus, I know how hard it has been for you to make a lot of these things, but you keep trying. So nothing nicer or better than seeing somebody who's down but keeps picking themselves up again and again in order to learn something new. I am really proud of you."

Chapter 16

I T HAD TAKEN a little bit to calm Mack down last night. After he'd gotten over the laughter, and she told him about what she'd done, he was angry. But the fact that she'd allowed Pengo to come and go without any issues made Mack look at her sideways. She shrugged. "I wasn't trying to cause him any trouble."

"But neither were you trying to do him any favors," he pointed out.

"I'm not sure that it has to be both," she pointed out. "I mean, obviously if something is going on, and this other poor guy did the time …"

"But he also did time for his own crimes, and so, while it's not necessarily something that we want to happen, I'm sure it's not unusual for somebody to get a B&E rolled into their other charges, even though they say that they didn't do it."

"Right," she agreed, "and I get that. Once you start protesting, nobody will listen to you anymore."

"Exactly," Mack confirmed. "So, sure, it's possible Brandon may not have done this one crime, but it'll be pretty hard to prove it."

"It's just the injustice of it all." He rolled his eyes. "I know what you will say," she interrupted, waving her hand at him. "If he hadn't done any of the crimes, it would be a different story."

"Yes, and I agree injustices make us mad and angry, and we don't like them, but they do happen," he pointed out.

She nodded. "And, of course, it wasn't in your jurisdiction," she reminded him, "so it's not as if you're responsible."

"I know I'm not responsible," he said, with a shrug, as he studied her. "That doesn't mean I want to see this go down in any jurisdiction. We do the best we can, but none of us are perfect."

"And I understand that too," she added.

And now here it was, the next morning, with the party tonight, but Doreen was trying to figure out just what she was supposed to do with the Pengo information. When her phone rang, she didn't recognize the number, but it looked somewhat familiar, so she answered hesitantly.

"There wasn't anything in here that mattered," Pengo stated in frustration.

"What were you expecting?" she asked, puzzled. "I said nothing much was there. It was just a file that Brandon was trying to get somebody to look at. Didn't I tell you all that before? Something about one of the charges that he had been charged with and I guess convicted of," she said, looking for the language she wanted, "but he didn't do that one crime, and it bothered him, and he was looking for the guy who did do it to be charged."

Then came an ugly silence. "Is that what you're trying to do?" he snapped. "Get me charged for something I didn't do?"

"If you didn't do it, then you won't get charged," she stated. "Why would you?"

"Brandon didn't do it, and he not only got charged, but he served time for it."

"Right," she agreed, "which is hardly fair."

"Wait, hang on a minute. What are you talking about?"

"I mean, he did the time, as you pointed out, and he shouldn't have."

"He also got off for good behavior, so it's not as if he really did *all* the time."

She frowned at that. "That's not the point. *Somebody*," she said, with emphasis, "got away with a crime."

"*Great.* Lady, do you know how many people in this town get away with crimes on a regular basis?"

"I really don't like to think about that," she replied carefully. "I was told this was a lovely town."

"Sure, it is a lovely town. Honestly, it's a great town," he admitted grudgingly. "But, if you're thinking that crimes have gone unnoticed and unsolved, you wouldn't be wrong."

"I'm sure there have been," she conceded, "and I'm doing my best to clean up what I can."

Another moment of silence passed, then he asked, "Is that what you're trying to do with me?" Then his tone turned ugly. "Are you thinking you'll stick me with some of these crimes that Brandon did?"

"I'm not saying that at all," she replied, "because, if you didn't have anything to do with it, then it's got nothing to do with you at all."

Pengo paused again. "I don't think I like this."

"Okay, so you don't like it," she said, "and I get that. I get that a lot actually. Though I'm really not sure why people get upset with me."

"Maybe because you keep interfering in their lives," he snapped.

She thought about that, even while he was ranting and raving. "I guess it is kind of interfering, isn't it?" she noted and then shrugged. "Oh, well."

"What do you mean, *Oh, well?*" he asked. "Brandon died. Isn't that enough?"

"The thing is, … did he have to die? I don't think so."

"What do you mean, *have to die?*" he asked in exasperation. "I mean, he served time, and he died, sorry. Too bad, so sad, right?"

She almost wanted to laugh at his rhyme, but it was obvious that he was angry at her for even bringing up such a suggestion. "It's not as if I expect you to confess or anything. A guy like you won't do that anyway."

"What do you mean, *a guy like me?*" he asked in a sharp tone. "There you go, already judging me, as if I've committed some horrific crime, and I haven't."

"Good," she declared, satisfaction in her tone. "Then you've got nothing to worry about."

"Look, lady. If you'll start interfering in my life, I'm warning you now. … Just stay out of it. Stay out of my life, stay out of my world, and stay away from me. I don't want anything to do with you at all."

"*You* called me," she retorted, "and *you* came to my house, *uninvited.* So obviously it's you who wants something to do with me."

"You can absolutely take me out of your mind right now. I don't want anything more to do with you, not now, not ever." And, with that, he ended the call.

If she was a little more thin-skinned, she would take offense at the way some of these guys talked to her. However, since she understood that they were more afraid than anything else, she was able to let them off the hook for their attitude and behavior.

When he phoned back a little bit later, he added, "I mean it. Stay out of my life." And he ended the call again.

She stared down at the phone and shook her head. *He's still the one who called her, so it's not as if she had to report it to Mack or anything.* But when she got a text from Pengo next, which repeated, **I mean it**, she responded with a text. **You're the one initiating all conversations with me, ... three times now. So obviously something is going on here.**

He phoned her back this time. "Get out of my life or else."

"Is that a threat?" she asked, with interest.

His tone turned ugly. "It wasn't, but, if you continue this harassment, it could be." And, with that, he ended the call again.

She wasn't even sure how *she* was harassing *him* because it felt as if he was the one harassing her. But she hadn't ever been in this position before and was pretty sure Mack wouldn't be happy with her. But then, that went along with everything else in her life these days. Just when she was trying to help people, everybody tended to take things the wrong way.

Shrugging, she put that out of her mind. Then she heard Nan in her head, nagging at her to wear a nice outfit for the Christmas party. Doreen sighed. Nan had been right. Doreen needed something special to wear to the party, and that was about to become an issue she would have to resolve fast. She still had some of Nan's clothes here, but was there something that she could wear?

She pondered that as she headed upstairs. This would be better than going shopping, or so she thought. She didn't know when she'd become somebody who hated to shop—maybe when she realized that her pocketbook money didn't reach the level of her previous credit cards anymore. Her husband had always insisted that she be dressed *properly*, and he always made the final call as to what *properly* meant. But here she was, trying to figure out something on her own, and it was exhausting to say the least.

She went through Nan's closet and found a black dress. Black might be okay but not for a Christmas party. It shouldn't be something with a funeral vibe, or at least that's what she thought Nan would say. The trouble with shopping in Nan's closet was that Nan liked bright colors, bold and dramatic. Yet not one red was among them or even a Christmassy-looking print. There was, however, a really deep forest-green dress.

She pulled that out and pondered it. Maybe if she had something to go with it, like a cream-colored jacket and matching heels, or she could even do red—but that might just make her look too much like a Christmas tree. She went through her closet and with delight pulled out a few of things she had saved from when she'd originally moved in. Sure enough, she found what she thought would be a really nice outfit.

Putting it on, she twirled around and smiled, then quickly took a selfie and sent it to Nan. Nan phoned her back, and she seemed a little choked up.

"Oh, my dear, you look absolutely lovely."

Doreen smiled and thanked the Lord because it had been one maddening task, and she was dreading the thought of having to do it all over again. "I was afraid you would tell me that it wasn't Christmassy enough."

"No, I think that'll be just lovely. I bought that dress so many years ago."

"Is it too old-looking, do you think?"

"No, that style has come back around, to be honest," Nan noted. "It's one of those timeless pieces you can just wear and never have to worry," she murmured. "A little bit of jewelry wouldn't hurt though."

"I'll take a look," she promised. "One more thing, Nan."

"Yes, dear?"

"I never found any mistletoe for the party."

"Oh, that's fine, child. As long as you are there, that's all I want." And, with that, she ended the call.

When a knock came on her door, she ran downstairs, and it was the courier with her grandmother's necklace.

Now Doreen wanted to wear it for the Christmas party, but, if she did, she couldn't surprise Nan with it for her Christmas gift, so that was out. But it did bring back memories of a couple other pieces she may have saved. They weren't expensive. They were just nice little pieces with more special memories than anything. One was a gold chain, made up of five strands together. She put that on and smiled. This would do just fine.

She quickly changed, put away her great-grandmother's necklace to wrap up later, headed downstairs, hearing another noise at the front door. Expecting it to be another parcel delivery, she walked over and opened the door without any warning. And there was Pengo.

He stood there, glaring.

She shook her head. "You're in danger of becoming a real bore. I get that you keep telling me that I'm the one who's bothering you, but the truth of the matter is that you're the one bothering me."

"I am not," he snapped.

"Hate to break it to you, but here you are on my doorstep yet again."

"I want you to leave it alone."

She frowned. "I'm not pushing it to begin with. I just wanted you to know that your friend was dead and look what trouble that got me."

"He wasn't my friend."

She stared at him and nodded. "That's obvious from the way you've been acting."

He flushed and added, "Look, lady. I don't want anything to do with this. I didn't have anything to do with the original crime, and I don't want anything to do with it now."

"Interesting," she muttered, studying him, but, the trouble was, she believed him. She sighed. "Okay, if you say you didn't, you didn't."

"So that's it?" he asked.

"Sure, I'm not pursuing this anyway. It obviously won't go anywhere," she explained, with a shrug. "However, if you do know something, it's definitely to your benefit to tell me."

"No way," he replied in a more relaxed tone. "You're just the type to pick it up and go cause trouble for somebody else."

"Somebody else who may have gotten away with murder?" she asked.

"Murder?" he gasped, and his eyebrows shot up. "Hey, who said anything about murder? That was a robbery, way back when."

"Yeah, it sure was," she conceded, "but your friend Brandon may have been murdered over it."

Chapter 17

PENGO SHOOK HIS head several times. "I had nothing to do with that."

"You keep saying that, and yet here you are on my doorstep again." He glared at her. "I know. I know. According to you, I'm just a pain in the butt."

"Yeah, you're not kidding," he snapped. "Why are you trying to cause trouble?"

"I'm not trying to cause any trouble, but it's been trouble for somebody else."

"But that person is dead, so it shouldn't matter."

She sighed. "Maybe, maybe not, but again, if you know something …"

"I'm not telling the cops nothing," he snapped. "They haven't done anything for me. I'm not doing anything for them."

"Fine, in that case, you can be on your way." She pointed to her front steps. "Don't fall. I haven't got any deicer yet."

He stared at her for a long moment. "I should fall and then sue you," he muttered, as he walked down the steps. He turned, looked back at her, and asked, "You'll lay off, right?"

"Will you lay off?" she asked him. "Because I only see one person continuing to make contact with me on this one matter, and it hasn't been me contacting you. I'm just getting ready for a Christmas party."

"Right," he muttered. "There's that big do at the retirement hall. My sister's going."

"It seems that half the town has been invited," she noted, with a wry shrug.

"I didn't get an invite," he mumbled.

She looked at him and smiled. "Do you want to go?"

"Heck no," he muttered. "The last thing I want to do is be locked up in a room with a bunch of old people."

"Yeah, I'm sure you don't," she muttered, "but, honest to goodness, they probably have more fun in their day than you do."

He took one last look at her and stormed away.

She laughed at that, knowing it was probably quite true. But his visit brought up something else completely unrelated, and that worried her. *Unrelated* and *worried* meant bad news somewhere along the line for somebody. She thought about it for a long moment and then looked back at Mugs. "What will we do about it, Mugs?"

He woofed several times and then lay down.

"You think we should just let it go, don't you?"

He woofed again.

"You're probably right. Plus, Mack would get pretty upset. Then, if we're late for the party, you know Nan would be very upset," And Doreen would do a lot to avoid breaking Nan's heart. And that's exactly what would happen if Doreen showed up late tonight. She groaned. "Fine, we'll get dressed and head down. I don't know if we're supposed to be early or what."

Nan would have a conniption fit if she thought Doreen would do something the *wrong* way. If it meant being early, you were supposed to be early. However, if you're supposed to be late, then you must be late. She sent Nan a text, asking if she was supposed to arrive early or late.

Nan phoned her back. "That's a silly question. It's a party."

"I know it's a party. That's why I'm asking you. I don't want you to be embarrassed because I don't know which way to go on this one."

"You would never embarrass me, child," she replied gently. "You can come anytime you want. I do know Mack will likely be a little bit late though."

"Fine," she muttered. "I'll be a little bit late too, so I'm not out of sync with Mack."

"Oh, that's good," Nan said, laughter in her tone. "It's nice to see the two of you so in sync."

Doreen did end up a little late getting to Rosemoor, just because the animals seemed way too excited. She was worried about taking them since there would be a massive crush of people. However, it also felt wrong not to bring her animals, when her animals deserved to be thanked too, as it wasn't just about Doreen. So she had to bring them. They were a team after all, and she was determined that they should be allowed to have fun and to steal the spotlight.

With a bow tie on Mugs, she made an attempt to pin a little Christmas ribbon bow on the back of Goliath's collar, and not to be outdone, Thaddeus was also sporting a little bow. She slowly started to walk down, wondering if she should have driven in this cold, and quickly realized it was way too cold to walk there. Heading back home, she moved everybody over to her car, and now finally loaded up, she drove to Rosemoor, only to discover it was almost impossible to find any parking. She groaned as she drove around, realizing she would still be a few blocks away, but that was the best she could do about it.

She hopped out, leashed up both Mugs and Goliath, then put Thaddeus carefully onto her shoulder, worried that he was already eyeing her shiny gold necklace a little too closely. He might end up embarrassing everybody if he decided it was something he should have. As she walked toward the front entrance, the doors opened immediately, as she was greeted with cries of well-wishes and Merry Christmas. She laughed as she saw both staff and seniors waiting for her. As she arrived, the cheers went up all around.

She shook her head, "Jeez, you guys. Come on. It's not as if you haven't seen me this week."

"Ah, but all this is for you," one of them declared, beaming.

"That's why I brought the animals. I truly hope it's okay."

"Of course it's okay. You and the animals are always welcome," the manager replied.

Doreen laughed. "I'm really glad you agree because I was worried about it."

"No, you and the animals are a package deal," the manager pointed out, "and we knew it. It's all good."

As Doreen walked in, she was surprised to see a couple standing in her way, hesitant, as if reluctant to approach any farther, unsure if they would even be welcome. Obviously they were welcome since they were here. With a closer look, Doreen noted it was Pengo and his sister, Miriam. She looked at him in surprise. "Look at that. You decided to come after all."

He turned and glared at her, but his sister shushed him. "Yes," she replied, looking over at Doreen, one eyebrow up. "I didn't think any animals were invited though."

"Ah, well, in that case, you would be wrong," Doreen stated cheerfully. "The animals go where I go. We're a team."

Miriam looked at her. "So, you're Doreen? The one that all this fuss is about, *huh*?"

"Yes, I'm Doreen," she confirmed, with a nod.

"I thought there was something familiar about you, but couldn't quite figure it out. What did you want my brother for?"

"To talk to him, but he seems to have gotten the wrong idea on the whole issue. I just wanted to tell him about Brandon. Now he's the one who keeps bugging me," she explained, turning to look at him.

"Hardly." He groaned, as he glared at her. "She's crazy," he added for his sister.

Miriam stopped, her eyes widening.

Doreen knew that look all too well by now. "Yeah, that's me," she noted cheerfully. "I'm the crazy lady who gets involved in all these cold cases."

"So you *are* trying to solve that case," Pengo stated, turning to face her.

"Except that you told me how you weren't involved. So, if you weren't involved, you weren't involved," she declared, with a shrug. "So, nothing else to say about it."

"Right, and I meant it."

"Of course. And I believe you."

"You do?" he asked, turning to look at her.

"Yes."

"Oh." He didn't seem to know what to say to that.

She laughed, then patted him on the shoulder and added, "It's all right, you know? Some people will believe you. Now go get some punch and relax, so you can enjoy the party." She motioned over to the side, where the refreshments and some snacks were.

"I haven't eaten all day," he muttered, warming up to the idea. He asked his sister, "Can I get you some punch?"

"Sure. I want to talk to Doreen for a minute."

He nodded and walked over to the refreshments table and quickly lost himself in the table of food.

Doreen watched him pick up food with both hands, and she laughed. "He really is hungry, isn't he?" She turned back to smile at the sister. "How are you doing?"

"I'm fine," Miriam replied, but her gaze was narrow and hard. "I'm just wondering why you're bothering my brother. You didn't tell me that you were looking at him as a suspect for a case. Had I known, I never would have pointed you in his direction."

Doreen shrugged. "I didn't know whether he had anything to do with it or not," she stated. "I was just asking questions. He says he didn't, so whatever. Besides, I contacted him to let him know about Brandon's passing."

"And that's it? You'll just believe him?"

"Yes, I'll just believe him," she repeated. She didn't elaborate about the fact that, as far as she was concerned, her inner guidance was pretty solid, and Doreen was a decent judge of character. Although Pengo was giving off all kinds of good vibes on the matter, Miriam wasn't. Doreen eyed Pengo's sister and asked, "Don't you believe him?"

She shook her head. "Of course I do. He's my brother."

"That's not an excuse though," she pointed out. "An awful lot of brothers out there are still criminals."

"Sure, but he's my brother, and I know him very well."

"Did you also know Brandon?"

She nodded. "I did. I have to admit that, back then, he didn't appear to be quite such a bad guy. It was really a surprise when he went down for all those crimes."

"And may only have been guilty of some of them. He admits he got into a bad way and had some bad friends who guided him in the wrong direction, but he left quite a few detailed notes," Doreen added cheerfully. "I haven't had a chance to get through them all."

"Notes?" Miriam asked faintly.

"Yeah, notes," Doreen confirmed. "He wanted to clear his name of at least one of the things he didn't do. He fessed up and pled guilty to the ones that he did, but he was adamant that he was innocent of one of them."

"Really?" Miriam asked, staring at Doreen.

"Yeah, really," she agreed cheerfully. "And then he died before he had a chance to do anything about it."

"So why would anybody care now?" Miriam asked, with a shrug. "I mean, he's dead."

"Sure, he's dead, and maybe a lot of people don't care, but I do."

"Of course you do." Miriam groaned. "It's that whole busybody part of your system, isn't it?"

"I don't even know what that means," Doreen admitted, looking at her. "However, I can tell you that, if there's an easy answer to this, I will try and find it."

"Why? Brandon doesn't care anymore."

"Maybe he doesn't care, but an injustice was done."

"Right, a busybody," she muttered. "Anyway, it's got nothing to do with me."

As she went to step away, Doreen stared at her and asked, "Are you sure?"

Chapter 18

DOREEN WATCHED AS Miriam froze in front of her, then slowly, oh-so-slowly turned to look at her.

"What are you talking about?" Miriam asked, her tone harsh.

Just as she spoke, the crowd noise had fallen into a sudden lull, so her words came across as unnaturally loud.

Doreen eyed Miriam in surprise, as people turned to look over at Doreen and the woman she was talking to.

Miriam flushed and glared at her. "Why would you even say that?" she asked in a hoarse whisper.

"I just wondered, since you seem to know Brandon so well." Doreen stared at Miriam. "I mean, you've got to think about what you do know and what you don't know. I would just assume that, if you already knew Brandon, you probably knew more than you expected to know."

Miriam shook her head. "That makes no sense."

"Lots of what I do doesn't make sense," Doreen admitted. "It just happens to be the way my brain works, which obviously is in a very discombobulated way."

"You're not kidding." Miriam stared at Doreen and added, "I don't want you saying anything that'll get me in trouble."

"Of course not." Doreen smiled. "That's not the intent."

"Are you sure?" Miriam asked. "It seems to me as if you're fishing."

"If I am fishing, what difference does it make?" Doreen asked. "You said you knew Brandon, and you knew him back before all this happened."

"Sure, but I didn't *know him,* know him."

"But you did," Pengo argued, as he ambled over, his mouth half full of food. "You guys even dated for a while there."

She stared at him. "Sure, but not for very long."

"It was over a year, if not longer than that," he pointed out to Miriam, frowning at her now. "You didn't even tell me about it. I had to find out from everybody else. It's like you kept it hidden," he said in an aggrieved tone.

She groaned. "It doesn't matter whether I told you or not."

"Except you just said you didn't know him."

"Then the question really is," Doreen interjected, "did you ever have anything to do with one of Brandon's shady business dealings?"

"Of course not," Miriam snapped.

"Yes, you did," Pengo countered, looking at her. "I mean, obviously it's been a long time, and you don't have anything to do with it now, but you did back then."

"No, I did not," Miriam snapped.

"Yes, you did. You used to fence some of his things, and that's how you got the money to start your fancy restaurant."

Doreen just watched in amusement as the sister tried to shut down her brother, who obviously had no issue with talking. Not to mention the fact that it appeared he had poured back a couple glasses of wine really fast, and already red spots were popping out on his cheeks. Doreen asked, "Enjoying the wine, Pengo?"

"I sure did," he said. "This isn't such a bad place to tank up. I feel as if I haven't had a decent meal in a while."

Doreen smiled at him. "And your sister? How has she been doing lately?"

"Oh, she's been making money hand over fist in that place of hers next to the food court. It's always been a good location."

"I *was* making money hand over fist," she clarified, "but things have been a lot tougher recently."

"You mentioned that before," he said, nodding, "but then you went and bought that house. I don't have a house," he muttered, glaring at her. "Heck, I don't even have a decent place to stay." He watched her ruefully, as if she were responsible for all the ills in his world.

Miriam groaned. "If you hadn't spent all your money left, right, and center, you might still have some to spend on a place to live."

"If you hadn't been given a lot of money from Brandon before he died, I would have had some money."

Another heavy silence fell around Miriam, as everybody gathered closer.

Doreen wasn't sure what was going on, but it was interesting. "Why would Brandon give her money?" she asked Pengo curiously.

"She gave birth to his son."

"Oh, so child support then?" Doreen asked.

"Yeah, child support," Pengo replied, "but I don't think it was his kid."

At that, his sister turned and snapped at him. "You just

shut up."

He laughed. "I mean, it was a good con, as far as cons go. A great con really. It's brought you all kinds of money over the years," he noted, with a smile. "I wish I was female, and I could pull a stunt like that. So many men end up paying for kids who aren't even theirs, and it doesn't even matter. They've got nothing to say about it." He laughed. "But, no," he added, talking directly to Doreen again, "Miriam's pretty smart when it comes to that."

"Is she now?" Doreen asked, trying hard to keep her smile off her face, as Pengo blabbed all of his sister's secrets. "I wonder if Brandon found out about it?" Doreen asked.

"Ah, maybe so," Pengo replied. "She told me how they had one huge fight."

"Interesting," Doreen murmured, as she turned and looked at the sister. "When did you see Brandon last?"

"None of your business." Her tone raised eyebrows all around them.

"She saw him the day he died," Pengo replied. "I know they were talking on the phone about meeting up in person. Brandon had a trip to do, and he needed to get on it."

"Interesting," Doreen noted. "That's fascinating." She turned to face Miriam.

"Yeah, he handed her a check for a bunch of money, but she wanted more. He told her how he didn't have any more. Yet he was going into business and was hoping that maybe it would be enough to pay his bills. How it was hard getting a day job when he had a record, which of course had started him off again on all the wrong things in his world."

"Of course," Doreen replied, willing Pengo to keep talking. "Plus, if he's paying child support and that's not even his child, that would hurt Brandon financially, not to mention the betrayal of it all. Especially since he'd already had betrayal on his mind, since he had to pay for a crime he didn't do."

"Exactly," Pengo agreed. "But that wasn't me, so don't you go putting that on me," he said in alarm. "I already told you about that."

"I know." She nodded at him, smiling.

Meanwhile, his sister was inching toward the main door. Doreen looked around to see how she could bring this to an end or at least get the answers that she was pretty sure were simmering just under the surface. Then she caught sight of Mack glaring at her, standing with his arms akimbo, blocking the exit. She gave him a beaming smile.

Miriam turned to look behind her and asked Doreen, "Who are you smiling at?"

"Oh, that's Mack, a very good friend of mine," Doreen replied, with a smirk.

Miriam hissed. "You have friends?" she asked, then gave an eye roll.

"Yep, I sure do," Doreen declared. "It surprises me too."

"Yeah, you're not kidding," Miriam muttered.

Doreen glanced at Mack, just shaking his head at the way the conversation was going. But Doreen wasn't quite done. She turned back to the brother. "Any idea if Miriam owns a gun?"

Pengo raised his eyebrows. "I have no idea." Then he stopped and frowned. "But, now that you mention it, Brandon did."

"As an ex-con, he had a weapon?" Doreen asked.

"Yeah, I told him it was a bad deal, and he knew it wasn't great, but prison had also taught him to be very wary. So Brandon felt better having it, though he didn't really know how to use it." Pengo laughed. "That was the thing about him. He was one of those guys who was always all-in, and it didn't matter if it made sense or not. So, when he got the call to do some of these jobs back then, he jumped." Pengo turned his sister. "Remember that job he did with the jewelry store? Brandon should never have gotten involved in that one at all." Pengo shook his head and laughed.

"Yeah, your sister arranged that one, didn't she?" Doreen asked Pengo.

"Yeah, she sure did."

"I did not," Miriam roared.

By now, everybody surrounded them, and Nan had her little book out and a pencil in her hand. Doreen shook her head. Her grandmother was probably taking bets on the outcome. Doreen groaned, not really expecting to have made quite this much of a scene at the party. Doreen mentioned to the group, "I'm sure it's something that someone would like to talk to Miriam about."

"I ain't talking to nobody," Miriam snapped.

"I still have a question." Doreen took a moment to stare down Miriam, then asked, "Do you still have the gun?"

"No, I don't have the gun, and I never did. And it was Brandon's gun," she pointed out. "I never used it."

"Yeah, you did," her brother declared, looking at her with his eyebrows up. "I taught you how to shoot myself."

"Did you now?" Doreen asked, with a nod. "You didn't happen to use it on the last day of Brandon's life, did you, Miriam?" Doreen asked, turning to look at Miriam with an eyebrow raised. "I mean, enquiring minds want to know and all."

Miriam stared at her. "Do you think I'm an idiot?"

"Nope, not necessarily," Doreen replied, "but I do think

you probably popped Brandon on that last day. He likely found out about your child support con, possibly from your brother here. All that money Brandon had handed over to you was money he needed now in order to survive himself. All that money paid for a child who wasn't even his."

"Maybe," she muttered, "on the child part, but I sure didn't kill him. He died in an accident."

"Oh, there we go," Pengo snapped. "*You* lied."

"I did not," she snapped right back at her brother. "You just shut up."

"You called me in a panic that day," he declared. Then his mouth gaped open and his gaze narrowed, as if it just hit him. "Did you shoot Brandon?"

"He died in a trucking accident, remember? You're such an idiot."

"Yes, he did," Doreen noted, "but he was shot first. I don't know whether you shot him while he was in the vehicle, or if you shot him and he hopped into the truck to get away, and in his panic, caused the accident. Regardless it was your hand on the trigger."

"You don't know anything," Miriam spat. "You can't prove that gun was in my hand. No way."

"It's at home though, if anybody wants to go check on it," Pengo shared, still staring at her. "Did you kill Brandon? Don't tell me that you did such a thing. That would be too awful to even consider."

His sister turned and stared at him. "Shut up," Miriam cried out. "Why can't you just keep your mouth shut?"

"Because, even for Pengo, murder would be a step too far," Doreen stated, staring at Miriam.

"Yes, it is bad, so bad, Miriam. You don't even have a kid, and you were cheating Brandon out of money. Everything you do is a con," Pengo wailed, raising his hands in frustration. "You're the one responsible for that B&E that got Brandon into so much trouble. He went to jail for you, for Christ's sake."

"Did you tell Brandon that Miriam did the B&E?" Doreen asked, turning to look at him.

"No, I didn't. She's my sister, after all."

"Right." Doreen nodded. Her gaze caught Mack's expression, as he stared at the couple in fascination. "But murder? That's a little too much to ignore."

"Yeah, murder is a *whole* lot too much to ignore," Pengo stated, turning to look at his sister. "I mean, you stole his money, but, jeez, you didn't have to steal his life." He glared at her. "Seriously?"

"He wanted to turn me in. He would make sure I paid," Miriam cried out, staring back at her brother as if willing him to understand. "No way I would do that."

"So, you just killed him then?" Doreen asked.

At that, she turned and glared at Doreen. "I ain't saying nothing."

"You already said more than enough," Doreen noted.

"Too darn bad because you can't prove anything." Miriam turned, looking for an exit, only to find Mack standing there at the door, his arms crossed as he stared at her. She turned back to Doreen.

Doreen shrugged and added, "This is Mack. He's a detective on Brandon's case."

Miriam gasped and paled, as her brother burst out laughing. "Good Lord," Pengo shouted. "After all this time you might have to pay for your crimes."

She turned on him. "What about *your* crimes?"

"Nothing I've ever done is anywhere near as bad as this,"

he declared, his smile falling away resentfully. "You had no business conning him out of child support for a child you didn't even have."

"He was the fool who paid up." Miriam sneered. "And that's got nothing to do with you."

"Yet it does, and you've always been like that."

"You're just angry that I didn't share."

He shook his head. "No. I wouldn't have wanted anything to do with that deal." He shrugged, as if shaking the bad mojo off him. "That's just wrong on so many levels."

"Oh, give me a break," Miriam snapped. "It has nothing to do with you, and you really don't care. You never did."

"Brandon was a really nice guy, Mir," he pointed out, obviously using her nickname, and his voice broke. "You didn't have to kill him."

"I did have to kill him to keep him from coming after me and opening up all these dratted cases," she snapped. "Even if I'd tried to pay him off instead, he would have known for sure it was me."

"It was you, so you should have just told him that and fessed up. You know your regular deal. Say you're sorry, pay him off, then sleep with him again." Pengo glared at her. "That's the normal trick you would pull anyway."

"I do not," Miriam snapped.

Pengo rolled his eyes at that.

Mack then took one step forward, and Miriam muttered, "Oh no, I didn't come here for this."

She started to back away, only to get tangled up in Mugs's leash. As she tried to step out of it, Mugs saw Mack through the crowd and raced forward, literally pulling Miriam's feet out from under her. She hit the ground with a hard cry and was dragged right up to Mack's feet, already hog-tied, rather like she was gift-wrapped, except she was missing the bow.

Doreen looked over at Mack and, with a smile, added, "Merry Christmas!"

He glared at her, but the place erupted with laughter. Unable to keep it in, Doreen exploded in a fit of giggles herself. "Merry Christmas, indeed," Mack muttered, glaring down at his suspect, neatly tied up in a dog leash at his feet. "Good grief, Doreen. You do know we were just supposed to come and enjoy a party."

"Yeah, I know, and I am sorry about that." She turned and looked at her grandmother. "I am so sorry, Nan."

"Oh, that's okay," her grandmother declared, looking absolutely thrilled. Then she turned to Mack and asked, "But you won't have to leave now, will you?"

At that, Darren popped up and offered, "I'll handle this. Don't worry."

Mack frowned at him. "You sure?"

"Sure, I'll get her booked at the station." Then he lowered his voice, though several people could still hear him, including Doreen. "You just look after my grandfather."

At that, Doreen turned to see Richie, a bottle of wine in each hand, dancing all by himself out on the dance floor. She started to giggle. "It's a deal, Darren. Thank you."

With that, Darren picked Miriam off the floor, quickly untangling her. "Yeah, I'm definitely okay to take in this one." He grinned.

Mack added, "I owe you one." Then he frowned, pointed to Richie, trying to snake dance now, waving the wine bottles. "Maybe you owe me."

Nan looked over at Richie and nodded. "You make a good point, Mack."

Looking alarmed, Mack looked back at Darren. "Nothing is ever simple when Doreen's around."

Darren laughed. "No, it isn't. Besides, you got something else you need to do here tonight. Right?"

Mack shot Darren a look but helped him escort the suspect out to the car.

When he stepped back inside, Doreen smiled up at him. When she saw the look on his face, she frowned. "*Uh-oh*, am I in trouble again? I shouldn't be in trouble. I didn't do anything."

"You didn't do anything?" he asked, his eyebrows shooting up high.

"Not really. I just talked her into confessing."

He thought about that and nodded. "I guess that's true, isn't it?"

"It absolutely is true," Nan stated, beaming. "She's really good at it."

"I know, but your timing could have been better." He looked over at her, with a sigh. "Fine, I won't get too upset at you this time."

Doreen nodded, then added, "See? I didn't get hurt this time. Nobody confronted me at home—well, except for Pengo, but he's harmless. So I did good this time, solving it in front of you, right?"

Mack rolled his eyes, grimacing at her.

"Besides, Mack, don't you have something you're supposed to do?" Nan asked, a big grin on her face.

"No." He glared at her. "I don't."

Richie danced over, wrapped an arm around Mack's shoulders and added, "Yes, you do. Yes, you do." Then he was pulled away by somebody to dance with them.

Doreen frowned at Mack. "What is it you needed to

do?"

"Nothing." Now he glared at her. "You definitely killed the mood."

"The mood?" she repeated, looking at him worriedly. "Are you okay, Mack? Are you not feeling well?"

"I'm feeling fine," he grumbled.

As Doreen took a step toward Mack, Mugs raced ahead and sat at his heels.

"What's the matter, Mugs?" Mack asked. Mugs gave several woofs at Mack, who looked down at him and asked, "What do you want now, buddy?" Nobody could figure out what Mugs was woofing about, and finally Mack turned to her and suggested, "You might have to take him out of here."

No sooner had the words escaped his mouth, when Mugs jumped up and hit him in the back of the legs, dropping Mack to his knees. Everybody laughed, and Mack glared as he straightened, but Mugs was having none of it. He raced around Mack, and Goliath, not to be outdone, quickly chased Mugs, now wrapping Mack up in two leashes, who then dropped to the floor again, on his knees.

Mack stared up at Doreen and asked, "Did you put them up to this?"

"No, I didn't do anything," she said. "I'm so sorry." She raced over and tried to help untie him, but it ended up with the two of them on their knees on the floor, facing each other, with her giggling and laughing out loud.

He wrapped her up in his arms, trying to contain his laughter, at the same time trying not to get fully knocked to the floor. "Nothing with you will ever be normal, will it?" Mack asked her.

She sighed. "I really hope you don't mind, but the answer would be no."

"Right." He shook his head and looked over at Nan.

Doreen got to her feet and tried to help him back up, but he said, "I might as well just stay here." He reached into his pocket, lifted up one knee, and asked, "Doreen Montgomery, will you marry me?"

She looked at him in shock, as the place fell completely silent. Mugs looked at her and woofed. Goliath howled. Even Thaddeus poked his head out from underneath her long hair and cooed, "Thaddeus is here. Thaddeus is here."

Mack looked at him and nodded. "I know, buddy, but we need her to answer my question."

Doreen looked at him, as tears started to run down her cheeks, and Mack seemed worried. She opened her mouth to say something, but the words just wouldn't come.

"You need to say something, dear," Nan suggested, with a smile on her face. "Otherwise Thaddeus will say it for you."

Immediately Thaddeus flung open his wings, smacking Doreen in the face, as he cried out, "Thaddeus loves Mack. Thaddeus loves Mack."

Everybody hooted and hollered, and Mack, still chuckling, finally said, "That's nice. I'm really happy you love me, buddy, but I really need her to have the same feeling."

Thaddeus looked at him, cocked his head from one side to the other side, then looked at Doreen and added, "*He, he, he*. Doreen loves Mack. Doreen loves Mack."

At that, Doreen unfroze and threw herself into Mack's arms, landing on the floor beside him. He didn't even get a chance to stand back up, as she just clung to him.

He managed awkwardly to get himself up on his feet and to pick her up, with the animals completely entwined around them, and Doreen cried out, "Yes, yes, yes."

The place erupted in a madhouse of cheers, and he leaned over and kissed her.

Mack was everything she had always hoped would be part of her future but hadn't really realized that her future was beginning right here in front of her.

Chapter 19

WHEN DOREEN WOKE the next morning, she had a beaming smile on her face. As parties went, it had been something else. Even Nan had called her late last night and exclaimed there would never be another party like it. And she congratulated Doreen several times, then thanked her for making Nan the best party-maker ever.

Doreen had barely even figured out what she was talking about, but apparently everyone enjoyed such a slam dunk of a time that it would go down as one of the greatest events the town had ever seen. And the fact that Doreen had somehow managed to solve an unknown cold case during all that madness had made it that much better.

She rolled over and grinned to see the animals all tucked up in bed with her, all the excitement of last night having completely worn the whole lot of them out. In the dim recesses of her mind, she heard her phone ringing.

She picked it up and saw it was Nan.

"Are you awake, my dear?"

"I am now, but the good news is, I woke up a few minutes ago."

"Oh, good. I think that was an absolutely fantastic party,

don't you? Shall we have another for New Year's Eve?"

"Oh, goodness." Doreen moaned. "It'll have to be a plain Jane party, without solving a cold case, if that's what you're talking about. I'm not going through that again."

"Are you sure?" Nan asked, disappointment weaving through her words. "It was such fun."

"Maybe, but I couldn't even begin to repeat that."

"Oh, we don't want to redo it at all," Nan explained, "but everybody voted this morning, and they were absolutely thrilled. Of course, there was also a betting pool set up for whether you would get a confession out of Miriam, and I'm happy to say Richie won that one. Then we had a really big Christmas pool as to whether Mack would finally get around to pulling the pin on that proposal, but the winner was Thaddeus, and we're all still really confused about that."

"How did that happen?" Doreen asked.

"We did allow for a couple people to come in from outside Rosemoor to put in bets for other people that they cared about. Thus the name on the winning card ... is Thaddeus."

After Doreen ended the call with her grandmother, she was revved up and happy inside, as she eyed the huge twinkling ring on her finger. Mack explained that he had it made from stones found among the cache of jewels they'd discovered at Mack's mother's place.

When his mom phoned a little bit later, Doreen was so thrilled and full of joy that she could barely contain it.

"Since the garden has not needed any work lately, I've been missing you terribly," Millicent shared. "I was so hoping to come up with an excuse to have you come visit, and yet I just couldn't come up with anything."

"How about you just tell me that you would like a visit?" Doreen suggested.

"But you are always so busy. Plus, you were hurt there for a while."

"I'm fine now, so how about I come over a little bit later today?"

"That sounds lovely," she cried out in joy.

After hanging up from that call, Nick phoned her and congratulated her.

"Did you know ahead of time?" she asked suspiciously.

He laughed. "I knew it was on Mack's mind. Apparently that was the real purpose for the party, so everybody could show up. And I know you won't believe it because you didn't see me there, but I was there too."

"No way. Were you?"

"I was, and Mom was too. We saw the whole thing but had to stay hidden or you might have figured it out beforehand. Yet Mom felt a bit under the weather, so I had to take her home early. Still, a part of me is incredibly jealous of the chaotic and overwhelmingly joyful life Mack will have with you. But another part of me thinks there's a lot to be said for peace and quiet."

She laughed. "And yet some of that stuff is completely overrated."

"It is, indeed."

When he ended the call, she got up, made coffee, then glanced outside and winced because it *looked* so cold. Only a few more days until the Christmas season was truly over, and then it would be a whole new year. She smiled as she thought about it. So much had happened, so many good things over this year, and she could never have imagined her life a year ago, ending up like this.

When she heard her front door open, and warm hands wrapped around her and tugged her up close, she leaned back and smiled. "Good morning."

"Good morning," Mack said, as he leaned over and kissed her on the cheek. His cheek was cold, and she laughed. "I gather it's chilly out there. I was looking to see if I wanted to step outside."

He chuckled. "No, I don't think you do. It's definitely on the chilly side this morning."

She nodded. "I can see that." She turned, wrapped her arms around him, and gave him a big hug. "There's fresh coffee."

"Now that is what I'm talking about," he said, as he let her go and walked over and poured a cup.

"I hope we don't have to make wedding plans anytime soon," she muttered worriedly.

"No. Not at all. No pressure."

"Are you kidding?" she asked. "Your mom and your brother have already called me this morning."

He grinned. "Yeah, they're both pretty excited."

"You're not kidding, and honestly, so am I."

He looked up, a broad smile on his face as he nodded. "Now that's good to hear."

"You won't stop me from trying to solve these cases, right?"

"No, I won't stop you from trying to do anything," he replied, with a headshake. "That's not the business I'm in."

She smiled and nodded. "So, do you have another case?"

"No," he stated, turning, his gaze narrowed at her. "I don't have another case."

"Okay, … I guess I can live with that."

"And you *can* live with it," he pointed out. "How about a deal? No new cases until the new year, okay? We'll have a nice, quiet Christmas."

"Sounds good to me," she muttered.

Epilogue

End of December …

"IT WASN'T MY fault," Doreen stated, as she glared at Mack. "You said we would wait until the new year, and I agreed to wait until the new year. It's not my fault that somebody just called and asked me to come over and look at his garden bed."

"What garden bed?" he asked in frustration. "And why do you want to go look at it?"

"Because he thinks a murder was committed on it."

He closed his eyes and whispered, "Dear Lord."

"I know. I know, but I didn't call him, Mack. I didn't have anything to do with it."

"You don't have to anymore," he noted, with a sigh. "They just seem to come out of the woodwork now."

"I know," she exclaimed, beaming so brightly. "Isn't it great?"

"And what do you mean, somebody was murdered in the greenhouse?" he asked. "Shouldn't he be calling the police?"

"Apparently it was a while ago, like a long while ago," she noted, nudging him, "so that should make it a cold case."

"Not if it's still on the books, it's not," he countered.

"I was hoping you could be more … considerate about that. I did call you, thinking you might want to come along."

"Yes, I definitely want to come," he replied, glaring at her. "I don't know why people always think they can go straight to you instead of the police." She didn't say anything to that, and he sighed. "You definitely get better publicity than we do."

She burst out laughing. "I do, and I'm sorry about that because I'm really not trying to make you guys look as if you don't do anything."

"That's exactly what it looks like," he declared. "Anyway, who on earth does he think was killed in his greenhouse?"

"He doesn't know. Supposedly—back then, a long time ago, when the murder supposedly happened—he found an awful lot of blood on this one garden bed. He says he took a lot of pictures, and he phoned the police right then. However, he hasn't been able to use his zucchini patch ever since then because he's been afraid it would destroy evidence. And well, I guess it just felt wrong."

"But he did contact the police?"

"He said he did, but it was a long time ago though."

"So, we don't know if a human body was there. We don't know who was killed there. We don't know who he contacted at the department. Meaning, we don't really know anything. *Great*. Another case bound to damage our reputation."

"But those were the old days," she noted, with a bright smile. "Not the new ones. Are you ready?"

"Ready for what?" he asked.

She smiled. "To start the new year, and to start a new year with … are you ready?" He nodded, yet with a sad smile. *"Zonked in the Zucchinis,"* she declared and burst out laughing.

After a few moments, it tugged a grin from him too.

She added, "Come on. Let's go. I can't wait to start a new year with you … and another round of cold cases." And, with their arms linked, they headed out to check out this case.

This concludes Book 27 of Lovely Lethal Gardens: Merry Mistletoe Madness.

Read about Zonked in the Zucchinis: Lovely Lethal Gardens Rewind, Book 1

Lovely Lethal Gardens Rewind: Zonked in the Zucchinis (Book 1)

Doreen is slowly recovering from the mad yet joyous ending to last year, as she faces the new year and what it might bring. Since she's now engaged to Mack—and everyone around her is pressuring her to pick a wedding date and hopefully soon—she yearns for another case to keep her busy.

So, when an older gentleman calls and needs help fulfilling his wife's last wish, Doreen is right there to help. The case is beyond cold, which means she gets free reign. However, when it starts to butt up against a new case Mack has, he's quick to move her back into her lane—only he's not quite quick enough.

Doreen and her trusty animal trio traverse the Joe Rich area to downtown Kelowna and back, as her cold case curls back around in on itself—and Mack's current case. Solving these two cases will be worthy of a mention in the history books!

Find Zonked in the Zucchinis here!
To find out more visit Dale Mayer's website.
https://geni.us/DMSZonked

Author's Note

Thank you for reading Merry Mistletoe Madness: Lovely Lethal Gardens, Book 27! If you enjoyed the book, please take a moment and leave a short review.

Dear reader,

I love to hear from readers, and you can contact me at my website: www.dalemayer.com or at my Facebook author page. To be informed of new releases and special offers, sign up for my newsletter or follow me on BookBub. And if you are interested in joining Dale Mayer's Reader Group, here is the Facebook sign up page.
http://geni.us/DaleMayerFBGroup

Cheers,
Dale Mayer

About the Author

Dale Mayer is a *USA Today* best-selling author, best known for her SEALs military romances, her Psychic Visions series, and her Lovely Lethal Garden cozy series. Her contemporary romances are raw and full of passion and emotion (Broken But … Mending, Hathaway House series). Her thrillers will keep you guessing (Kate Morgan, By Death series), and her romantic comedies will keep you giggling (*It's a Dog's Life*, a stand-alone novella; and the Broken Protocols series, starring Charming Marvin, the cat).

Dale honors the stories that come to her—and some of them are crazy, break all the rules and cross multiple genres!

To go with her fiction, she also writes nonfiction in many different fields, with books available on résumé writing, companion gardening, and the US mortgage system. All her books are available in print and ebook format.

Connect with Dale Mayer Online

Dale's Website – www.dalemayer.com
Twitter – @DaleMayer
Facebook Page – geni.us/DaleMayerFBFanPage
Facebook Group – geni.us/DaleMayerFBGroup
BookBub – geni.us/DaleMayerBookbub
Instagram – geni.us/DaleMayerInstagram
Goodreads – geni.us/DaleMayerGoodreads
Newsletter – geni.us/DaleNews